Sister Ambrose at Close of D:

Sister Ambrose closes the sh
keeping the last of the light from the mo
stars shut outside in the cold and dark and
standing back crossing herself from forehead to
breast from shoulder to shoulder with her middle
digit remembering the first time she entered the
convent and saw the high walls and locked doors
and long cloisters and the chill that seemed to be
forever in her bones no matter the time of year or
season and Sister Bernard gazing at her with a
combination of sternness and boredness as if it
all meant nothing any more this welcoming of
new girls to the convent this taking in of new
recruits as Sister Josephine called it and thinking
of the first time she dressed in the habit and put
on the undergarments that were as sexless as
dead meat and feeling the roughness of the black
serge itching her skin and boots heavy and
corked soled for silent walking and never run
anywhere Sister Bernard said always walk as a
nun ought as you have seen them in the cloister
and church entering and leaving and as she now
walks to the bed and begins to undress from the
stiff habit she thinks of her mother's pale skin the
last time she saw her the cancer already then
dragging her off to a certain painful death the
eyes haunted the lips thinly drawn across her

mouth and her father standing beside her his eyes watery his droopy moustache like that of Nietzsche his hands held tightly in front of him an old rosary hanging there unused but prayed upon once by his mother in her long life and Jacques her one time fiancé standing the other side of her mother supporting her holding with his strong hands his eyes studying the one he once loved and now had lost forever behind the high walls to a God he didn't believe in but cursed all the same and now putting on her nightgown she pushes all thought of Jacques away all memories of their love making all reminiscences of that last summer she puts at the back of her mind where it occasionally pushes itself out and haunts her and having dressed in the nightgown she sits on the bed and taking the black rosary from the bedside table with its lamp and book of prayers and chamber pot beneath in the small cupboard she begins her prayers rubbing her thumb over the Crucified feeling His body beneath her fleshy thumb sensing His head all the time the words leaving her lips like escaping birds from opened cages sometimes she feels she has angels at elbow and foot at other times she senses demons at ears and tempting her fingers to pleasure her flesh and as she moves on to the beads smooth and round like black peas allowing her eyes to wander from the wooded floor boards with its scrubbed clean look to the bookcase with bible and books on prayer theology philosophy poetry a worn copy of The Imitation of Christ and letters of St Therese of Lisieux and the old armchair where she had placed her habit and the dark well worn crucifix on the wall above her bed with the Crucified hanging there His head to one side with a crown of thorns and the closed eyes shutting out it seems to her (as her words continue to flow from her tired lips) all that is happening in the room and in the world and in her aged heart the arms stretched out across the wood nails hammered home in the hands and closing her own eyes pausing her prayers and words she imagines her soul and that of her sisters in Christ rising up on the last day and up and away like unleashed birds of prey.

Matins 1907.

The bell from the cloister rang. Echoed around and settled upon nun in bed cosy under blanket against morning's cold and frost. Stirred. Head raised. Eyes peered into the dawn's light, sighed, shivered, moved arms against body's length. Closed eyes. Wished for more sleep. None to have. Bell rang. *Time, ladies, please.* Time and tide. Stirred again. Lifted head. Sighed. Gazed at bedside table. *Clock tick-tock, tick-tock.* Moved to the edge of the bed. Feet dangled. Toes wiggled. Hands joined for prayer. Breath stilled. Silence of the room. Bell stopped. Sighed. Breathed air, cold air. *Wake up, rise, and shine.* Funny words. Tired still. Wished to sleep, but no time. Dangled feet rose and fell. Toes wiggled. Rose from bed and knelt on wooden floor. Hard floor. Cold floor. Polished to a shine floor. Knees slid on smooth surface. Back stiff from straw-stuffed bedding. Sighed. Sister Teresa joined hands. Let fingers touch. Let flesh touch flesh. Sin on sin once maybe. Long ago. Sighed. Opened eyes. Gazed at crucifix on wall above bed. Old Christ, battered by time and grime. Eyes closed image held in mind's eye. Prayer began. Words searched for amongst the wordless zones. Reaching through darkness for an inch of light. Light upon light. Darkness upon darkness. Who felt this she does not know. None speaks except Sister John. Word upon word built. Holy upon holy. *Sit here*, she'd say. *Rest a while. Rest in cloiste*r. Rest on bench by cloister wall. You and she. Her hands old and wrinkled by time and age.

Her eyes glassy. Her voice thin and worn, yet warm. *Want to be close to warm. Especially in dark cold mornings like this*, Teresa mused, lifting head and opening eyes to dawn's light and cold's chill in bone and skin. She stood and dressed. Dis-robed from nightgown and into habit. Black as death with white wimple of innocence. Laughed softly. Such times. Such times. Harsh serge against soft flesh. Stiff whiteness on skin's paleness. Sighed. Coughed. Made sign of cross from head to breast to breast. *Never to touch*, Mama said, *never let be touched.* Words, long ago. Mama is dead. *Rest in peace.* No mirror. No image of seventeen-year old face or features now. Vanity of vanities. Sighed. Papa said, s*ome men would deceive. Deceived by what*? She often asked, but none would tell. *Ding dong bell.* Silence now. Go now. Moved to door and down the cloister to the church and the dawn's welcome cold and still. Teresa closed door and walked at pace soft and motionless seeming. None shall speak. Sing and chant and raise eyes and maybe a smile briefly, *but none shall speak. Nor touch. For none may touch. Not as much as a sleeve felt or breath sensed. Each one an island.* Water upon water none shall cross. Teresa sighed. Walked down the steps one by one, not to rush, but not to lag sloth-like, lazily or drag wearily. Mother Abbess would know. Knows all. Sensed all. Next to God most feared. Most loved maybe if truth were known. Teresa sighed. Chill of cloister ate at bones and flesh. Nimble walking might ease, but walk as nuns do and cold bites like violent fish. Breathed in the air. The moon still out. Stuck out on a corner bright and white. The sun's colour fed the dawn's light. Brightness promised. Warmer weather. *Warmer than Sister John. Who knows,* Teresa mused, touching the cloister wall for sense of touch. *Absence of touch can mean so much,* Jude said, years before. Jude's image faded now. No longer haunting as before. Teresa brushed her finger on the cloister wall. Rough and smooth. Rough and smooth. *Men may deceive,* Papa said. *Let none touch,* Mama advised. Long ago or seeming so. Seventeen-years old and innocent as innocence allowed. Jude laughed, feeling such. Wanting to touch. Over much. Entered church. Cool air. Sense of aloneness. Choir stalls. Smell of incense and polish mixed. Sense upon sense. Smell upon smell. Walked slowly. Genuflected to Christ. High on high. All seeing. Like Mother abbess. But less human. Less human all too human. The Crucified for all to see. Half naked there. Stretched wide arms. Head dangling lifeless or so seeming. Genuflection over moved to place in choir stall, stood, and stared at vacant wall. Brick upon brick. Sounds held. Chants upon chants sang once, held here. Chill in bone and flesh. Breviary held. Pages turned. Find the place and mark it well. Bell pulled sounds now. Nuns entered and gathered round. Sister upon sister, elbow near elbow, *but none may touch. None may touch. None may touch.* Sister Rose eyes dim searched yours for morning joy. Smiled. Coughed. Awaited tap from Abbess. Smiled. Nodded. Hands held beneath black serge. Wanting to hold something, someone, but none may do so. None may touch. Tap, tap, wood on wood. Chant came as if from the cold air settled on ears. Felt in breast. Sensed and blessed, but none may touch. The sense to sing. The voice raised. The ear tuned. The mouth and lips employed, but none may touch. *At least,* said Sister Rose, n*ot over much. Not over much.* Still air. Cold air. Warmth wanted. Sister John or Sister Rose. None shall touch.

Lauds 1917.

Light from window in the refectory touched the eyes of the nun standing by the table. Memories touched. Opened like a box of tricks. Not knowing is the trouble, not knowing. Stood still. Hands clutched the white mug. Solidness and coldness. Whiteness of a sepulchre. Death-like. Plato came to mind, but was soon dismissed, sent packing. Gone now. Only room for God in the mind. The light opened a door. The door creaked. Years ago, a girl saw something. *Was it I?* Sister Teresa asked. However, knew it was. *Shut the door. Shut the door.* The light ought not to let in such memories. She pressed her thoughts back into the tight box of her brain. She lifted the mug to her lips and sipped. Warmness, sweetness, touch of home long ago. Closed her eyes. Tried to lift to prayer. *My God where are you?* The light sat on her eyelids. Waited for them to open. She squeezed tight shut. The eyes seemed almost liquid; tears lingered on the rims. The door tried to open. The girl saw. *Close it out,* she said. The light teased her. The eyes opened and welcomed. Light from light. And near by another nun lingered in the corner of her eye. Large as lard; black serge against the light of day. Murmured prayers. *Touched hands. Not to touch, not to touch overmuch.* Warm tea. Mug lowered. Mouth sour; lips opened to prayer, but none came. *Where my God?* She placed mug on the table. Hard table, wooden table, well scrubbed and clean. Plato tried to enter. Send him packing, him, and his philosophy. Bell rang from bell tower. All are still. Echoed bell. *Shall all be said to be as death*? Nearby nun moved, her serge swished and swashed. Others moved. She remained. She remained. What can be gained? The light from light. The God from God. Sister Teresa moved. Mug lifted and taken to the kitchen and washed. Each thing in its place, each place for its thing. Ring the bells. Ring the bells. The nuns are moved. The light is left. The prayers wait to be ignited. To be lifted up. She entered the cloister. Coldness lingered about her limbs. Her hands folded themselves beneath her cloth. Her feet placed their steps. The soft touch of shoe on stone. The bone against bone. The girl stood by the door and saw. Nuns surrounded her. The church door opened and all entered. Two by twos. Fingers touched from stoup to finger to finger and breast to breast. Holy cross made. Each to each their place they took in silence. All is silent. All but breath, mumbled prayers, coughed up lungs, clicking tongues. All is opened to the light of the church windows. Light from light, touch to touch. Not to touch. Touch not. Not overmuch. Settled in choir stall. Gathered thoughts held in check. *Jude dead now. Passchendaele claimed him*. So Papa wrote. Ink black. *Death where is thy victory*? She sighed deep. Knew it was as had to be. Jude dead. His hands touched her once. At night, she can still feel the warmth in dreams. She lifted her eyes to the windows. *What memory can fade?* Jude was once, but now rose up like the Crucified to haunt her mind and heart. Papa said *men are not to be trusted. Men are such creatures. What is man that you are mindful of him? Back in the box such thoughts.* The Abbess knocked wood on wood. Broke from her thoughts, Sister Teresa bowed her head and neck like one to be executed. Off with her head. Off now with Jude's head, or so was written. Papa writes so neat. Black on white. Death's fingerprints on a dead man's sheet. Sighed. Held breviary tight. Opened to the page. Eyes touched paper, seemingly so. Thoughts lingered. Prayers were said. Chants lifted to above their heads. Not to touch, not to touch. *But only if such touch could heal a wound,* she mused, turning the page, felt the paperiness beneath her finger. She sighed. Prayer seeped in and seeped out. The light from light dimmed in the church. The Crucified hung at the altar end. Silent and unspeaking. *Forgive them,* He might murmur, Sister Teresa mused darkly as she turned a page. She felt the undoneness of her Christ. She felt the bone tear from bone and flesh from flesh. She pushed her feet deep into her shoes against the cold. Her fingers stiffened. The page white and black. Death's stinginess against life's sweet pail. Sing, sing, and sing. However,

do not touch. Do not touch, least not overmuch,
Sister Rose had said. Gone now. Fled the walls
for the World's foul touch. Men are not to be
trusted. Least not overmuch. Now and at the hour
of their death. All death. Each death. Until death,
they do part.

Prime 1927.

Sister Teresa put down the pen. Eyes searched
page. White and black. Scribbled words.
Meaning there some where amongst the lines,
she mused. Bell rang from bell tower. Echoed
around cell. Closed her eyes. Held hands
together. Sighed a prayer. Allowed the dark and
peaceful to swim about her. *Out of the depths, O
Lord,* she whispered. Opened eyes. Parted hands,
rested on the table before her palms up, and read
the signs. The last echo went out of the room.
The whisper of it out of earshot. First-class now
this age; first-rate her papa had thought; foremost
her mama decided. *Gone now Mama*, she mused,
lifting her body from the chair and walking to the
window. Gone except memory. What the little

child had seen she wanted to forget. Some memories are best buried. The sky was cold looking; the clouds shroud-like. Held hands beneath habit; clutched hands child-like. Mumbled prayer. Watched nuns move along cloister; watched the slowness; sensed the coldness of the air. *If possible,* Lord, she murmured, moving from window, walking towards the door. Paused. Looked back. Stared at crucifix on wall. The Crucified agonised, battered by age and time. Smiled. Nodded. Turned and opened the door and walked into the passageway. Closed the door with gentle click; hid hands beneath the cloth; lowered eyes to floor's depth. Wandered down by wall's side. Listened. Sighed. Sensed day's hours; day's passage and dark and light. Entered cloister and felt the chill wind bite and snap. Best part, Papa had said. *Men are not to be trusted,* said he many a time. Felt the cloister wall's roughness with her right hand. Sensed the rough brick; sensed the tearing of the flesh on wall of brick; the nails of Christ. Mama had died her own crucifixion. The child closed the door having seen in the half-dark, she recalled, closing her eyes, feeling the chill wind on her cheek. Paused. Breathed deep. Saw sky's pale splendour; saw light against cloister's wall; saw in the half-light. Nun passed behind. Sister Helen, big of bone, cold of eyes, cool of spirit. Cried once; cried against night's temper. *Months on months moved on; days on days succeeded.* Papa had said, the zenith of the passing years, *my dear child, your mama's love. How pain can crucify*, she thought as she moved on and along the cloister, lifting eyes to church door. Nails hammered home to breast and ribs, she murmured as she entered the church. Fingers found stoup and tip ends touched cold water; blessed is He, she sighed. Eyes searched church. Scanned pew on pew; nun on nun. Sister Bede nodded; held hands close; lifted eyes that smiled. Where Jude had been buried, Papa had not said. Ten years have gone past; time almost circle-like, she mused, pacing slow down aisle to the choir stall. Sister Bede lowered her head; lowered her black habited body. Saw once as a child but closed the door. Poor Mama. *Who is she that came and went?* Long ago. Time on time. Papa had missed her; tears and tears; sobs in the mid of night. Mother Abbess knocked wood on wood. Silence. Closed eyes. Dark passages lead no where, Papa said. Chant began and echoed; rose up and down; lifted and lowered like a huge wave of loss and grief. Where are you? What grief is this? Night on night, her papa's voice was heard; echoed her bedroom walls; her ears closed to it all except the sobs. *De profundis. Out of the depths. Dark and death are similar to man and child.* Opened eyes to page and Latin text. *Bede and she, to what end?* Death, dark, and Mama's fears echoed through the rooms of the house; vibrated in the child's ears; bit the child's heart and head. *This is the high poin*t Jude had said; had kissed her once; had held her close and she felt and sensed. *Men are not to be trusted.* Breathed deep. *For thine is the kingdom.* And Papa's words were black on white and pained her. Jude gone and buried; Mama crucified; Sister Rose fled the walls; wed and wasted to night's worst. *Come, my Christ*, she murmured through chant and prayer; c*ome lift me from my depths; raise me up on the last day.* Voice on voice; hand on heart; night on night. Jude had said *be prepared for the next meeting*, but dead now; Passchendaele claimed him. Voice on voice, Amen. Chill in bone and flesh. Breath eased out like knife from wound. Bede looked and smiled; hid the hands; bit the lip. *Men are not to be trusted.* Jude long gone. Nuns departed. Bede turned and went with her gentle nod. Paused. Sighed. *Come, my Lord and raise me up,* she mused, stepping back from stall and the tabernacle of Christ. R*aise me up. Raise your lonely bride from death and dark.*

Terce 1937.

Blessed art thou amongst women. Sister Teresa
closed the book. Brushed hand across book cover
dispersing dust and thoughts. *And blessed is the
fruit.* She lowered her hands to her stomach and
tapped three times. Empty tomb; empty womb.
Looked across the room at the Crucified hanging
on the white wall; hammered and nailed; battered
and bruised by time. She brought her hands
together. *Let flesh touch flesh.* Jude long gone, in
flesh at least. Papa had gone the year before; no
last farewell; no last goodbye. Sighed. Lifted her
eyes to the off-whiteness of ceiling; lifted her
heart and mind to a world beyond. Bell rang from
bell tower. Voice of Christ, some said. Closed
eyes. Held breath. Then released breath as if God
had touched her afresh. *Men not to be trusted,*
Papa had said. Last will and testament; his last
words, she mused. She rose from the table and
book; stood gazing at the black book cover; stood
in a silence like one struck dumb. Bell rang.
Sighed. Moved across the room; opened the
door; closed it with softness of summer's breeze.
Mama wore black in perpetual mourning. Black
on black; death on death. She moved along the

cloister; touched the wall; felt the roughness of brick on brick. Jude's image pale as ghost; off to her right she thought he lingered. *All in the mind,* Mother Abbess had said; smiled; patted her hand. *Not to touch, not over much.* She paused by church door and felt for the stoup; dipped finger in water; hoped for blessedness; made sign from breast to breast; scanned the choir stalls for Sister Clare; not there, she mused; disappointment stabbed her; drove her inwards; struggled with her night of soul. *And blessed is the fruit of thy womb.* Jude kissed her once or was it more? She mused, taking her place in choir; shifting her breviary; clutching it tight. Nun followed nun; each to their own place; each to their God prayed, she mused, opening the page, shifting her weight from foot to foot. Mother Abbess tapped wood on wood; made the sign from shoulder to shoulder; nodded the beginning of prayer and chant. N*ot to be trusted,* Papa had said. Not seen last nine months; sorely missed; huge chasm in her breast and heart. Turned the page. Lifted her voice. Eyes flowed across the black and white as if swimming through the sea of despondency. No Sister Clare. *I do declare a pain is here; wish you were here; near me now*, she said inwardly, following the words like lost sheep. *Where are You now my God?* Sighed. Held the breviary; felt the weight of it; like her sins it weighed her down. Sunlight shone through upper windows; touched the stone floor between choir stalls; made as if fire burned between them, she mused, letting eyes move from the page; allowing memories to stir like giants waking from slumber. Flesh on flesh; hand on hand to touch. Not over much, not over much. *And where are You?* she asked in her silence; settled her feet in stillness. *Pray for us sinners. Now and at the hour. Where had time gone?* Papa gone; Mama long since dust to dust; Jude blown to the four corners in battle; all so sorely missed. No Sister Clare. Chant ended. Silence. Mother Abbess made sign; blessed all gathered; gathering her black robes she moved slowly down the aisle with her bride groomed but invisible Christ and the sisters followed each too with their battered and bruised groom inwardly held; separately loved. Sister Teresa waited and watched. Knelt and sighed. *Where was her groom? Had He gone or died*? Closed eyes. Sighed. Brought hands together; moved lips and mumbled prayer, which lingered just above her head; blessed the air. Now and at the hour.

Sext 1947.

Il dio è il miei testimone e guida, Sister Maria,
the refectorian, had said, Sister Teresa
remembered walking past the refectory, touching
the wall with her fingers. *God is my witness and
guide*, she translated, feeling the rough brick
beneath her fingers. She stood; turned to look at
the cloister garth. Sunlight played on the grass.
Flowers added colour to borders and eyes, she
thought, letting go of Maria's words as if they
were balloons. Ache in limbs; a slowness in her
movements. Age, she muttered inaudibly. The
war had taken her cousin's sons in death. Two of
them. Peter and Paul. Burma and D-day. Three
years or more since. She brought hands together
beneath the black serge of her habit. Flesh on
flesh. Sister Clare had touched. Not over much,
not over much. Papa would lift her high in his
arms as a child, she mused, her memory jogged
by the sunlight on the flowers. Higher and
higher. Poor Papa. The spidery writing
unreadable in the end. She sniffed the air. Bell
rang from church tower. Sext. She looked at the
clock on the cloister-tower wall. Lowered her
eyes to the grass. So many greens. *Jude had lain*

with her once or was it more? She mused, turning away from cloister wall and the sight of grass and flowers. Thirty years since he died. Blown to pieces Papa had written. Black ink on white paper sheet. Flesh on flesh; kiss to lip and lip. She paused by church door; allowed younger nuns to pass; so young these days, she thought, bowing, nodding her head. Placing her stiff fingers in the stoup, she made cross from breast to breast. Smell of incense; scent of wood; bodies close; age and time. She walked to her place in the choir stall, bowed to Crucified tabernacled. Kneeled. Closed eyes. Murmured prayer. Heard the rustle of habits; clicking of rosaries; breathing close. Opened eyes. Sister Clare across the way. A nod and a smile, almost indiscernible to others, she thought, returning the same. Mother Abbess tapped wood on wood; chant began; fingers moved; sign of cross; mumbled words. Forty years of prayer and chant; same such of fingered rosaries; hard beds; dark night of soul and such. She sensed Papa lifting her high in thought at least; Mama's touch on cheek and head. Jude's kiss. Embrace of limbs and face. *Il dio è il miei testimone e guida,* she recalled: *God my witness and guide.* Closed eyes. Sighed. Sister Clare had cried; had whispered; witness and guide; witness this and guide, she murmured

between chant, prayer, and the scent of incense
on the air.

None 1957.

Afternoon sun touched the cloister garth. The
office of None had just completed. Sister Teresa
walked slowly down the cloister from the church,
letting her failing eyesight search for the opening
to the garth. Heard the clink of cups on saucers;
the chatter of voices; nearby the smell of the
flowers in the flowerbeds. Her white stick tapped
against the wall as she walked; her arthritic hand
gripped it painfully. Felt the sun's rays on her
face; the slight breeze touched her habit like a
saucy child. Remembered a summer long ago
before she entered the convent. The green of
grass in her memory and a kiss. *Who's kiss?* She
searched her memory like one seeking through
an old chest. *Jude. Yes, Jude.* Smiled. Felt
opening in the wall; turned into the garth. She
remembered vaguely his face; felt the grass
beneath her feet. Someone touched her arm with
their hand. One of the sisters spoke. Not Sister
Clare. Dead now. Most of them were she knew.

She listened to the tone of the voice; her eyes failed her again. Sister Mark. Her mind grasped the image that fitted the voice. She smiled. Sister Mark had led her by the arm and asked about tea and cake. *Tea, yes, no cake,* she said. Mama had a similar voice. Mama had said *not to let them touch. Not men; not to be trusted.* Or was that Papa? She couldn't remember. *Take it easy,* Mother Abbess had told her; *take things steady.* Fifty years since she came that summer. She recalled the heat of that summer. The cloister's smell of bread and incense. Papa's face when she left home that day; the tears in his eyes; the awkward smile on his lips. No one came now. All dead and buried. Clare in the convent cemetery next to the wall; mole holes along by the gravestone. That had been an adventure in the art of love. A secret known only to God and them. Mea culpa, she whispered. Sister Mark handed a cup and saucer; soft hand touched hers; sweet voice spoke of the weather and the smell of the flowers. Sighed. Breathed in the air. Sipped tea. Cup rattled in the saucer. Stood here once and spoke to all; now few speak; only the kind and brave. Sister Mark spoke of the new novices and of the freshness about them. Sister Teresa looked about her; a vague scan of images; of faces in white and their youthful giggles and chatter. She had been as such once. She, her loves, and her memories. The bell tolled from the cloister clock; voices stilled. The breeze calmed. The sun eased off and hid behind a cloud. Someone took her cup and saucer and placed a hand on her arm. *Not to touch, not over much.* Mama had said. One of the dead. The God blessed dead. She walked back along the cloister, the hand still on her arm; flesh on flesh. Not to touch, not over much, a soft voice whispered of long ago.

Vespers. 1967.

Sister Teresa felt the cold evening wind through the cloisters. Shadowy figures sounded near by; the sense of waiting; the held breath; the stillness before the office of Vespers. She refused the wheelchair; wanted to walk along the cloisters to the church. A novice sister held her arm to guide her; Sister Bernadette's young hand on her elbow. Blind now apart from shadows and imagined faces from memory. She sighed. Sensed touch of the novice's hand. Breathed in the evening air; remembered the years of waiting in the cloister; the anticipation; the prepared prayers; the youthful voice gone now, she mused, releasing a breath-like prayer. She recalled Sister Clare's embrace by the wall where the cloister bell-rope hung like a tail. *God is my witness and saviour,* Sister Maria had said. She's dead too, Sister Teresa, thought, peering through her darkness at the shapes and figures ahead. Was it Jude who had kissed her once or was it more? She wasn't sure. Time distorts, she muttered softly, but none took notice. She breathed the air; sensed the dampness; the evening prayers hung in the air of yesteryear. The novice squeezed affectionately; her whispered voice soft and child-like. *Did she need the toilet? Was that what she said?* Words carried off in the air like the dead friends of her contemplative life. She shook her head; squeezed shut her eyes until lights flashed behind them like a stormy night. Whether the novice was pretty or not, she had no idea; had no sense of her except the touch of hand or softness of voice. *Papa was in his heaven, but Mama where was she? Do not let them touch she had said; men are such creatures. Flesh on flesh; lip to lip.* Jude had kissed and lain with her, she thought through her muddled mind. Clare had held; dead and buried; her mole-tilled ground holy still, she wanted to say, but only sighed. Movement. Bodies moved. Sister Bernadette touched her arm; gently prodded onwards; said gentle words; failed to keep hold of; slipped away like soap in a bathtub. She tried to clutch the passing words, but silence returned black and deep as the darkness of her days and nights. Chill in the air. Sighed. The footsteps on stone; the echo of chants surrounding as she moved to the pews reserved once for the lay-sisters, none now, all left or dead and swept away like the dead leaves of autumn. She sat; uttered the prayers; listened for the soft voice of the novice nun; wanted to feel; to hold; to *touch. Not too much, not overmuch. God be my witness and saviour,* she whispered between prayers and chants, recalling a kiss, an embrace, but not of Judas, not of Judas. She breathed the chill air; imagined Clare was there; imagined Christ's breath on her cheek and brow; a light far off beckoning from a distant hill.

Compline 1977.

Converte nos, Sister Teresa whispered, leaning forward in the darkness of the church; convert us, she repeated, sensing the infirmarian nun beside her, hearing the breath and muttered prayers. She had insisted on being wheeled into the church for Compline; had got her way; was pleased she was in the pew where she'd sat for the last ten years. She loved the silence before it all began; the sense of space; the soft opening of the Confiteor, the movement of bodies like a wave of water over the blacked-out walls and high roof of the church. She brought her arthritic hands together; dug deep for a fresh prayer, but all was used; all had been done before; all spread wide over her life of contemplation; in and out of her light and alternating darkness. The infirmarian muttered something. Sister Teresa shrugged her shoulders; inclined her ear; moved her head and unseeing eyes. *Was it Sister Bernadette? Or was it another?* She couldn't tell; all were the same in her darkness, except the touch; hand on hand; whispered words. Long ago, Jude or Judas had kissed; had betrayed. The sound of footsteps on flagstones; the rustle of habits and clicking beads; a sense of breathing and life; entering into the shared darkness and blackness, except for the red altar light to inform of the Crucified's presence and the all-seeing-eye. Sighed. Waited. Held breath. Reached for the sister's hand or arm to reassure, to sense she was not alone in the dark and that she had not died and sunk to dimness and damnation of another dark. The infirmarian tapped her hand. Relief. Converte nos, she mumbled, convert us, she repeated. The Confiteor opened up as if the whole world had breathed out in one voice; had poured out the world's sins in a soft eruption of voices. She breathed in. Clutched her hands. Wanted the closeness and nearness of all; wanted to be held; to be kissed; wanted to see the face of the sister beside her who sat close and whispered her own Confiteor. Ora pro nobis, she whispered, pray for us, let me not be lost in this darkness. *Where was Papa? Where is Mama? Clare where are you?* she muttered, her eyes searching the blackness, reaching out with a hand into the empty space before her. Hand on hand. Whispered voice. The chant rose and fell like a gentle sea carrying the prayers of the black-robed sisters. Jude or Judas and the kisses and betrayal. Dead now; all dead; all gone. Left here, she muttered, like a beached fish, flapping on the emptying sands of my hourglass like a whimpering child. She clutched her breast; sensed a pain. Leaned her head neatly on the sister's shoulder; sank slowly into her arms like a child searching for its mother's breast and the comforting embrace of warmth and love. Stillness. Peace. Darkness. Light.

The Tempest of Sister James.

The bell rings from the cloister. Sister Ignatius opens the shutters of the infirmary with an unfolding of her arms, as if she were about to dance, as if steps of some ballet were on her mind. You watch her from your bed, watch her arms unfold and spread themselves outward.

Morning, Sister James, the infirmarian nun says, moving to your bedside with a slow glide. You say nothing, but your eyes want to speak, want to say: *Oh what a bright day.*

The nun moves on to another bed and says: *Morning, Mother Margaret.* The other elderly nun murmurs words, but they are lost on you, as if carried off by some wind.

Hey, my hearts! Cheerily, cheerly, my hearts! you say, lifting yourself from the pillows. The nun returns smiling, she smoothes your brow.

Be with you in a minute, Sister, she says.

Tend to the master's whistle, you say.

Won't be long, Sister, the infirmarian says, moving to the other nun who needs her aid.

Sister James is in good spirits, today, Mother Margaret says, moving herself awkwardly to the side of her bed. The infirmarian nods and helps Mother Margaret to the chair beside her bed.

A young nun enters the infirmary and stands by the door.

Sister Elizabeth, tend to Sister James. We are to take them both down to the church; Mother Abbess has requested it, Sister Ignatius says with a hint of a sigh.

The young nun moves to your bedside, her plump face bringing a welcome.

Morning, Sister James, she says. You gaze at her, at her plump features, her eyes magnified behind her glasses. *How are we today?*

Blow till thou burst thy wind, you say. The nun smiles and helps you sit upright and moves you to the edge of the bed.

Does she remember her days as Choir-Mistress? Sister Elizabeth asks, lifting you carefully into the wheelchair by the bed.

Seems not to, Sister Ignatius replies. *Seems lost in her youth as a young actress. She was quite good, so I have heard.*

An actress? Gosh, how marvellous, Sister Elizabeth says. She wheels you to the sink and begins to wash your face. There is a certain gentleness about her, a calmness. *How long has she been a nun?*

She came in 1938 at the age of eighteen, Sister Ignatius says. She begins to help the elderly nun to undress, to remove her nightgown, and undo her other garments.

She must be the oldest nun here, the young nun says, easing the flannel over your face, wiping your brow.

Sixty-six years here and eighty-four years old, Sister Ignatius informs.

There use to be Grand Silence when I was abbess, Mother Margaret says grumpily.

There still is, Mother, but here in the infirmary we have permission to speak, Sister Ignatius says, helping the nun to wash herself.

*I forgot, M*other Margaret confesses, *I forgo*t, she adds, a look of sadness skims over her features, floats over her eyes. *Forgot,* she repeats, *forgot.*

The bell rings again. It echoes around the cloisters and seeps through the windows and into the infirmary. There is a mild movement in dressing, in preparation. The time is come. The hour is here. The Lord calls.

After mass, you are wheeled into the cloister garth and placed beneath the cherry tree out of the sun's heat. Sister Elizabeth settles you, gives a smile and leaves for other duties somewhere else, far beyond your knowledge or understanding now.

Flowers are spread around the border; their colours, smells and beauty are not lost on you, though words do not come for you to state such things or label things as once you would. The cherry tree is like an old friend, its old branches spread out over you like protecting arms and fingers. You may have remembered it being planted if time were not just a mass of days lost in a dark fog. You notice a nun working along the border at the top end, her black habit making her like a large crow digging for worms in the earth. You do not remember her name. Names are here and gone. They float pass you like summer butterflies. The sun warms your face; the sunlight makes you lower your eyes. Your hand moves to your lips, wipes away dribble. The nun stands by the border, stretches herself, gazes over at you, but your eyes stare down at the grass. Something about the grass, its greenness, its smell, draws your eyes towards it. *There was grass once*, you think you recall, *the smell of it fresh cut, where you and another sat, but who it was whom you sat beside is* withheld from you, just a memory lost, just a memory lost.

Nice morning, Sister James, says Sister Norbet, standing over you in the wheelchair. She smiles nervously, as if she were concerned you may suddenly reply.

The sun's enough to warm even the coldest heart, Sister Henry says walking up from the border.

Whose cold heart? Sister Norbet asks.

A mere saying, Sister Norbet, a mere saying, Sister Henry informs. She moves beside your wheelchair and peers at you. *She loves the sun*, she adds, tapping your hand gently as if you were a child.

She's wrapped well in case it should turn cold,
Sister Norbet says. She stands upright and looks
over the green cloister garth. *She seemed happy
to be in church today. Nice for her and Mother
Margaret to be in church for mass.*

Mother Abbess thought it best, Sister Henry says.
*Even if they cannot take part fully, their mere
presence is good. A real community of sisters.*
Sister Henry gazes at your lips where a small
dribble sits. *Those lip*s, Sister Henry muses, *sang
so lovely once, a voice of an angel, the Holy
Father once told her years back.* The dribble
moves and hangs over your lower lip. *She met
the Holy Father in the 1980s.*

How marvellous, Sister Norbet says. *I wonder
what he said to her?*

*He was overwhelmed by her knowledge of
Plainsong and her voice, inform*s Sister Henry
studying the dribble hanging like a dewdrop.

*Such knowledge she ha*d, Sister Norbet says.
*Gone now. I wonder what she remembers? Do
you think she remembers such things?*

Who knows. States of mind are an enigma.

Somewhere in her mind such memories may still reside asleep. Sister Henry pauses, moves her gloved-hand and wipes the dribble from your lower lip. You raise your eyes to the nun whose rough gloved-hand has touched you. She smiles a stiff smile. Her features do not register, do not click. You look away; move your head to look across the cloister. Their words disturb you, buzz about you like summer flies.

You taught me language, and my profit on it is, I know how to curse, you say suddenly, lifting your eyes to the sun.

We need no curses, Sister James, Sister Henry says. *She often speaks such things.*

I don't know what to reply, says Sister Norbet. *I seem at a loss.*

She was an actress before she entered the convent. Some say she could have done well, but she chose Our Lord. Sister Henry pauses, gazes at your head, at the way your profile has aged. *Her memory of the stage remains strong, as if part of her still remains there.*

Why speaks my father so urgently? you say. Sister Norbet bites her lower lip. She is uneasy.

Your father has only your rest at heart, Sister
James. *Rest your eyes*, says Sister Henry
kneeling by the wheelchair, patting your hand.

Did you know her father? Sister Norbet asks.

I humour her. Her father has long since died,
Sister Henry says.

This is strange, you whisper to Sister Henry.

What's strange? Sister Henry asks.

I must obey, you say.

Obey whom? Sister Norbet asks leaning forward.

My lord Sebastian, you whisper, lowering your
eyes to the grass again.

Who's Sebastian? Sister Norbet asks.

I've no idea. Some memory, perhaps, Sister
Henry says. The two nuns stand over you gazing
at your lowered head.

Seawater shalt thou drink, you say, waving your
hand by your cheek. The nuns move away. Sister
Norbet to her tasks elsewhere and Sister Henry

back to the border along the cloister garth. The crows have gone. The sun warms you, as if a kiss touches your upturned cheek, as if a memory awoke in you.

Sister Scholastica takes you to the toilet and after a small meal break returns you to the cloister garth, where you sit once again beneath the cherry tree. The sister crouches by your wheelchair and gazes warmly at you. Her features are familiar, but familiar to whom, you forget. A light makes a small opening in your memory, but it closes again.

Wonderful day, Sister Scholastica says to you. The cherry tree provides just the right amount of shade. She looks up at the tree, her eyes catching a sparkle of sunlight. You look at her with a determination to converse, to make some connection.

Remember I have done thee worthy service, told thee no lies, you say quietly. Sister Scholastica turns and lets her eyes move over your features. There is a warmth there, you notice, a gentleness, but who she is you cannot recall.

You have done us marvellous service, Sister

James, and told us no lies, the nun says.

Made thee no mistakings, served without or grudge or grumblings, you whisper.

You have served us and God so well, Sister Scholastica replies. She stands, places her hands on the arm of the wheelchair and looks at you.

How's our senior nun today? Sister Thomas asks, moving on to the cloister garth.

She seems well, Sister Scholastica says. And conversing in her own way. Sister Thomas comes to the wheelchair and bends down. Her large eyes peer through her glasses and settle on you like butterflies.

*I miss her not coming into the library, s*ays Sister Thomas. *I have her own books still on the shelf.*

She has contributed so much to the knowledge of plainsong, Sister Scholastica says. You look out across the cloister garth. Your ears hear their words, but it is all babble. Your hand moves to touch Sister Scholastica's hand. She smiles and taps your hand gently. *Whose hand was it that I held once?* you muse, looking at the hand tapping your own. *Whose hand? So long ago.* A long passage of time. You close your eyes. The voices are silent now. Only birds sing. And a soft breeze touches your cheek, like a slight brush of a hand. *Whose hand? Whose hand? Whose hand?*

After lunch, Sister Rose pushes you in the wheelchair along the path to the shore at the far end of the convent grounds. Sister Jude, the seamstress, walks along side, her hands tucked away in her habit. Your head shakes side to side like a puppet as the wheelchair travels over the uneven path.

Sister Perpetua asked me to take her down to the shore to watch the ships pass by, Sister Rose says, her face stern, as if she'd heard bad news. *She makes me uncomfortable when she says things. I've no idea what to say in reply.*

Who? Sister Perpetua? says Sister Jude.

No, Sister James, Sister Rose replies moodily.

I seldom see her, Sister Jude says, *only now and then in the refectory or in church.*

*She comes out with all sorts of thing*s, Sister Rose says. *I don't understand her. I feel out on a lim*b. Her arms are stiff; her eyes stare out at the horizon.

Best to humour her, Sister Jude says.

All well for you to say, but I'm the one who has to cope, Sister Rose moans. You grip the sides of the wheelchair as the rocking gets worse.

O, it is monstrous, monstrous! you say. Sister Rose stops pushing and leans down beside the wheelchair.

It's the ground, Sister James, not me, Sister Rose says.

The winds did sing it to me, you say. Your eyes lift and gaze at the young nun beside the wheelchair. A*nd the thunder, that deep and dreadful organ-pipe, pronounced the name of Prosper.* Your eyes scan the features of the nun, but nothing comes of her name, or who she is, or if she means good or bad. You look away and stare down at the grass.

See what I mean? Sister Rose says. What can I say? *And who is Prosper?*

Memory is a strange thing. Maybe someone she knew years ago, Sister Jude suggests smiling at you, as if you were some pet cat who needed words.

I wish she'd sleep, better for me if she does, Sister Rose says. She pushes on; her arms rigid, the wheelchair swaying like a ship at sea. You close your eyes. The sway sickens you, as boat rides always *did when you were a child. A boat, you muse,* like *the one I was in whenever it was, if ever it was,* you think, unsure of what or when it was the boat came into it all. The sway is the same. The sickness also. And *who was the captain? Whose boat?*

The two nuns pause by the shore and set the wheelchair facing the sea. You smell the saltiness, feel the breeze, hear the gulls above you, though you do not look up, but open your eyes and set them over the horizon with its greenness and blueness.

She was a great choir-mistress in her day, Sister Jude says.

I've only known her like this. Hard to imagine her otherwise, says Sister Rose, looking down at your head, slightly tilted.

She was well-known for her knowledge of plainsong, Sister Jude informs.

And now reduced to this. I feel uncomfortable. How can it happen to one who was so bright and clever? Sister Rose says lifting her eyes from your head, staring out at the sea, as if she looked for an answer amongst the waves.

Things happen, Sister Jude says quietly. *Her mind maybe muddled, but her soul is what matters to God. The quality of her soul, not her mind is what matters to Him.* Sister Jude stares down at you, wonders how much you hear and understand, how much is now lost to you.

He does hear me, and that he does, I weep, you say emotionally.

Does she speak of God? Sister Rose asks, turning to gaze at you.

Who knows of whom she speaks. We can only imagine it is God, says Sister Jude, bringing out her hands from her black habit, putting them gently over yours.

You feel the touch of her hands on yours. The face does not fit where it should. Faces come and go like shadows in and out of dark passageways. *Whose face and whose hand? Whose? Whose?*

How fine my master is! you say suddenly. *I am afraid he will chastise me.*

I'm unsure what to say, Sister Rose says.

Humour her, Sister, humour her, Sister Jude suggests.

You will not be chastised. Your master loves you, Sister Rose mutters. She bites her lower lip. She is anxious of her own words. She does not know why or from where the words came. She becomes silent.

You recall a hand, a boat, a face in the sunlight, but whose? Whose? Whose?

After the office of None you are wheeled into the cloister by Sister Blaise, she positions you so that you can see across the cloister garth. Her hands come together beneath her habit like lost friend. She stands beside you, her eyes settling on your profile like bumblebees on a flower.

Best place to be, says Sister Augustine, walking slowly towards the nuns, her walking stick tapping beside her. *I have always loved this part of the cloister.*

Sister James can see all from here, Sister Blaise says. Her eyes can follow the sisters as they pass, can watch the birds in the cloister garth and enjoy the flowers in the borders. Sister Augustine sits on a small bench along the wall of the cloister, her aged bones bending awkwardly.

Now she must rest, but once she seldom sat and rested, Sister Augustine says.

I've heard she was a bundle of energy in her younger days. Now she is a prisoner of incapacity, Sister Blaise says.

We are all prisoners of our bodies. She, however, had many options before she became a nun, says Sister Augustine.

*Options? a*sks Sister Blaise.

*She was a young actress with a bright future. She was much loved by Lord Sebastion Propero who used to take her out in his yacht, and if she married him would have been Lady Miranda. She told me of the large picnics they had on the lawn of his large house and how he had proposed to her th*ere. Sister Augustine pauses, stares out across the cloister garth, catches sight of Sister Henry bending down in the border. She remembers the days when she too bent amongst the flowers in the border, breathing the smells and scents.

She gave up all that for God? asks Sister Blaise.

She said she had her Road to Damascus experience while on the yacht one day and decided there and then that she would become a nun, Sister Augustine informs.

What did Lord Propero say to that? asks Sister Blaise.

He thought her mad, she told me once. Even her father was against her entry to the cloister. He wanted the match to be settled, wanted his daughter well married and away from the stage. Sister Augustine pauses again for breath. She gazes at the rising form of the nun in the border, at the rising form spreading out her arms like a scarecrow. *She entered at eighteen with no one's blessing, with nothing to gain but God's blessing and maybe...* Sister Augustine pauses again for breath.

She must have had a strong will, states Sister Blaise.

Only in doing what she considered God's will. In herself, she was passive. She sought nothing that was not in the pursuance of the will of God. She has paid the price of aged flesh and mind, but her soul is God's, says Sister Augustine.

You lift your head to the sound of the voices. The faces are familiar, but to whom or where you fail to remember. Your hand rises to your lips and wipes away dribble. Your eyes move away from the nuns to the cloister. The sunlight has become weaker; a mild breeze enters the cloister.

I fear a madness held me, you say quietly. The nuns turn to gaze at you. Sister Augustine frowns at your words.

Not madness, Sister, a tired mind, she says.

If I have too austerely punished you, your compensation makes amend, you whisper to the elderly nun beside you. Sister Blaise looks away, unsure of the words. Sister Augustine takes your hand in hers and gives a gentle squeeze.

You taught us well, Sister Augustine says. *Your wisdom still resides within us. I remember those things.* She gives your hand another squeeze.

Now my charms are all over thrown, and what strength I have's mine own, which is most faint, you say closing your eyes. The nuns gaze at your lowered head and closing eyes. Sister Blaise frowns, peers at your profile as if attempting to solve a dark mystery. Your head drops forward, the chin resting on the black cloth of your breast. You sense darkness overwhelm you, a slight light dims to your left. You sense a sinking into emptiness, as if falling endlessly through numbness.

Feel for a pulse, Sister Augustine says releasing your hand. Sister Blaise reaches through the black cloth and fingers for a pulse, but finds none. She shakes her head. Her eyes widen and a sense of panic rises within her.

Best go find Sister Ignatious, I will stay with her, Sister Augustine suggests calmly. The nun takes flight along the cloister like a disturbed blackbird, her arms almost flapping her to flight. Take rest, sister, take rest, your hour has come.

There is a small stir in the cloister. Black figures move like crows to a feast. You are still now. Your body slumps at rest. Sister Augustine stares into the border of flowers. She smells the scent of flowers and death.

Shrove Tuesday.

Sister Scholastica walked slowly from the church along the cloister and paused by the wall. The sun was warm; birds were singing from the mulberry tree in the cloister garth. Shrove Tuesday. Pancakes. Sister Benedict mentioned them after mass. Sister Scholastica remembered her mother making pancakes in the lucid days between her bouts of insanity. They reached to the full span of the dark pan she used. *Speak to me, Mother*, she used to say when her mother's madness gripped her tight, but she never did or rarely if the mood took her, Sister Scholastica mused, brushing her hand along the cloister wall with the rough bricks. She sniffed the air. Flowers. The sunlight caught her face; warmed her. She hid her hands beneath her black habit; moved away from the wall; walked along the cloister towards the refectory. Her stomach rumbled softly. Hunger. Lent soon. Less to eat. She recalled her mother's eyes when the madness held; the darkness; the anger and fear. Her father took her for the last visit to the asylum, the summer ending, the clouds dark that day. She never spoke; just stared out at the fields beyond, as if an answer lay there she could not reach. The refectory door was open. Sisters gathered by the breadboard. Softer mumblings; stomachs rumbling. Sister Scholastica cut her slice of bread; walked to her table; waited for the abbess to knock on wood. Her father had been too strict; too hurtful, especially after mother's madness showed, and after, when she'd gone and the large house seemed empty. The abbess knocked; the sisters chanted the grace; then sat on the long benches that lined the tables. The nun reading began her drawn out book on some dull saint from a dusty book from the library, her voice dry as paper, and her eyes following the page lazily. The Crucified hung from the wall above the abbess's chair; His arms strained with the sins of the world; His eyes pleading to the ceiling, which was stained, and dark. She ate the dinner; watched her sisters; wondered who would be the first to go or die amongst such few. Sister Dominic had died a week ago; found huddled in her bed; stiff as the stick she used to hobble round with clickedy click, clickedy click. Pancakes arrived. Hers was thin; rolled and touched with sugar and lemon. She cut and ate slow. Allowing the taste to simmer on her tongue as it had as a child. Francis had wanted only sex;

he never really loved her; just led her on for months on end. The last copulation a dark affair, unwanted and haunting. The pancake almost dissolved on her tongue; the lemon touched and tingled. The pancake had gone. The plate empty. She sat; listened as the reading nun droned on. She placed her hands beneath her habit; felt her breast beneath the cloth; the softness still there. The sunlight touched through the high windows; sprinkled on to the tables and floor; the Crucified hung in His lonely silence, His arms out stretched to embrace the world of dark and bright. Never saw Mother again; never knew her embrace once the madness came. *Father, forgive me for I know not what I've done*, but still the beatings came; the locked room for hours and hours; the only light, the small chink through the drawn curtains. The abbess knocked; the sisters rose; the grace chanted; the sound of prayers spoken; the touch of hand on hand beneath the black habit as the refectory emptied and was left to its silence once again. Sister Scholastica paused by the wall. Sniffed the flowers; breathed in the air; felt the sunlight kiss her brow as Francis did, but far more warmly, more constant, more loving, she mused, lifting her face to the sun letting the memories drift off like the birds in the distant trees over the cloister walls.

Ash Wednesday.

The priest thumbed ash on Sister Scholastica's forehead, his thumb firm like that of Francis whom she thought she loved once. *Memento homo, quia pulvis es, et in pulverem reverteris,* the priest whispered. Her mind translated the words her father use to relate often in his foul moods, *remember that you are dust and to dust you shall return;* then he'd beat her for some misdemeanour she'd forgotten from days before. The dirty ash made her feel as if she was marked out again, that her father would come rushing through the church doors, grab her with his mighty arm and beat, and beat. The priest had a lean face; eyes deep as if they had been set back too far. His lips slits in his paleness. She moved back to her place in the choir stalls; knelt down sensing the first day of Lent biting at her stomach already; the days ahead and hunger; the mark seemed to burn; she wanted to rub it off as she did as a child once and her mother said she would be damned. Her mother used charcoal to draw; once drew the Crucified in such detail that it made her cry. In her lucid days, she would paint for hours, before the madness swung her back and forth in and out of sanity like a pendulum. Through the slits of her fingers, she watched Sister Cecilia kneel as if stabbed in the back; the eyes glaring at the cross; the hands tight together in tormented praise. She'd seen her once, kiss the statue of the Virgin in the cloister, and whisper words. *Faith in words; faith in words.* Sister Scholastica heard the bell sound, rose, and stared at the priest at the altar. Mass. Bread and wine. Body and blood. Broken and spilt. Francis had not loved her as he said, just in it for the copulation and the image of her on his arms to impress his friends. Wednesday. It had been a Wednesday when they copulated the first time back in her youth; the grimy bed, which she remembered, had the smell of cigarettes and beer and days of being unmade. She lifted her eyes to the Crucified. His arms outstretched to embrace the world; His head to one side as if listening to her every thought and whispered word. Repentez-vous et le péché pas plus, Sister Gabrielle had said once when she was a girl at school, regret and sin no more, she'd repeated to them in her broken English. Innocent days. Mother swinging from lucidity to madness like the censer boat the altar boy swung at mass. Sister Scholastica closed her eyes. Her father raged in her memory at her mother's growing madness; her mother painting a red cross on the bedroom door; cursing her husband in French at the top of her voice. Peace now. Lent has begun. Sackcloth and ashes. Sin on sin. Washed away with the blood. Monthly bleeds; the blood of the Lamb. Requiem in pace.

Maundy Thursday.

Sister Scholastica left the refectory after lunch; made her way to the grounds for the twice-daily recreation period. She had been one of the twelve nuns to be chosen to have their feet washed by the abbess later that day. Some were too old, some too young, she imagined, looking for a quiet spot to wander; take in the scenery; meditate on her day and the following days to come of Easter. A chaffinch flew near by; a blackbird alighted on the ground and then flew off again. She paused. Maundy Thursday. Her sister Margaret had died on a Thursday. She remembered the day her sister was found in her cot by her mother; heard the screams; the rushing of both about her; her father's harsh words; both shouting; she being pushed aside; wondering what had happened; no one saying until the small coffin was taken out of the house for the funeral and off to the church which she was not allowed to attend. Mother was never the same afterwards. The days of lucidity grew less and less; madness crept over her like a dark spider spinning its web tightly. She sighed. Walked on through the grounds, walked past the stature of Our Lady green with moss and neglect. The sun warmed. *Say your prayers,* Mother had said, a*lways say your prayers.* Mother's dark eyes lined with bags through lack of sleep, peered at her especially when the madness held her like a bewitched lover. *Poor Margaret, poor sister, only said baby sounds, off into the night.* One of the nuns passed her with a gentle nod and a smile. Sister Mary. She saw her once holding the hand of another sister, late evening after Compline, along the cloister in the shadows. Father fumed at the creeping madness; Mother's spewing words; the language foul. She stopped; looked at the apple orchard. *Le repas saint: le corps et le sang de Christ,* Sister Catherine said to her that morning after mass, *the holy meal, the body and blood of Christ,* Sister Scholastica translated in her mind as she paused by the old summerhouse. Francis, who once claimed to have loved her, wanted only to copulate; left her for some other a year later. A bell rang from the church. Sighed, Time not hers. She fingered her rosary, a thousand prayers on each bead, each bead through her finger and thumb. Her father beat her when her mother's rosary broke in her hands; the room was cold and dark. *Pray often,* Mother said, in moments of lucidity. Time to return. The voice of God in the bells. She turned; walked back towards the convent, her rosary swinging gently in her hand, her eyes taking in the church tower high above the trees; a soft cool breeze kissing her cheek like Francis did once, long long ago before Christ called and made her a bride; clothed her in black as if in mourning for the sinful world she'd left behind.

Good Friday.

Sister Scholastica waited in the cloister with the others nuns. The mass in church was soon to begin. She looked briefly into the cloister garth; caught a sight of the spring flowers in the flowerbeds; a robin was on the far off wall. Sister

Gabrielle stood in front of her, her black habit neat and dark like an enormous rook. She recalled her mother baking hot cross buns; tapping the bread with a knife in the sign of the cross; smiling with the beginning of the madness just lingering behind the eyes. She sighed; looked around at the nun's head; at the sloping shoulders; at the way the arms were tucked inside the habit out of sight. Sometimes at night she dreamed of her dead sister Margaret; dreamed of seeing her smiling face amidst the fair curls of her head like small cherub; then the face would vanish; a skull would appear and she would cry out into the dark night of her cell and then try stop herself before the others came running as they did once before. She fingered her rosary in her inner pocket, moved her finger over the beads. The bell rang from the bell tower; the nuns moved on into the church in pairs, each placing their fingers into the stoup of holy water; making the sign of the cross over their black breasts. She smelled the incense; saw Father Gregory to her right waiting with Father Dominic; remembered his mumbling voice at mass the day before; how she understood very little of what he said. She took her place in the choir stalls; turned facing the altar with the huge Crucified hanging nailed to the dark cross His eyes closed, His lips slightly open as if calling out in a soft whimper. *Christ è morto per voi,* her mother would say, in the Italian she broke into when she was angry or overtly religious as she was in her days of looming madness. *Christ died for you,* her mother would repeat in English, as if in desperation that her daughter should understand. Father never understood; he never said he loved me; never once embraced me when I needed comforting when they took Mother off to the asylum. He would stare into space; there would be that contempt in his eyes, for me, for Mother, for God whom he said he hated even though he'd lost his faith years before. The mass began, the chanting voices rose; the church filled with the smell of incense, bodies, wood, old damp stone; voices riding up to the high windows. *Good Friday. Father hanged himself on a Friday, two months after I entered the convent. Dark days. Black nights. Christ died for us,* for Father with his stern temper and smacking hand and fiery eyes, for Mother and her mind undone at the seams and her eyes dark and gazing at the far off hills for some saviour amongst the crows. For Margaret whose stiff white body lay for hours in the cot smelling of urine and faeces. She sighed. Stood and watched, as the priest raised his arms and in her mind's eye cringed, as if expecting her father's hand to swoop down through the dark cloth of the priest,

and beat and beat and cast her down into the cold
dark room for hours crying into her hands;
caressing her body as if it were Christ's, and not
hers, that shivered in the purgatory of her father's
cruel making. Good Friday. Here. Saved.
Blessed. Amen, she whispered, behind her hands
as she knelt in prayer; her mother's ghostly
image knelt beside her; giggled like a school girl
tickled and tumbling in the far away clover of her
grandfather's lands in Italy.

Holy Saturday.

Sister Scholastica entered the church; sat on one
of the choir stalls gazing at the Crucified up
above the altar. Incense lingered from mass
earlier in the morning, merging with the smell of
old wood and damp stone. She rubbed her rosary
between finger and thumb. The arms of the
Crucified seemed taut; the head leaned to one
side with eyes closed as if dreaming of a paradise
soon to be realised. *Sabbatum Sanctum,* she
whispered, sniffing the air, feeling the smooth
beads between her thumb and finger. *El cordero*

salva a las ovejas, Sister Maria, the Spanish nun
had whispered to her the previous evening as she
sat in the cloister after Vespers. *The Lamb saves
the sheep*, the nun had repeated in her broken
English, smiling softly, a sparkle in her dark-
brown eyes. Her father, she remembered, pulled
a wooden crucifix from the wall and threw it in
the fire cursing all and sundry for her mother's
onslaught of madness. The crucifix burned; the
Crucified blackened in the licking flames. Too
harsh, her father was, the beating too frequent.
Pater Noster, she whispered, moving the black
beads through her fingers, feeling in her memory
the cruel blows. Her mother bought Easter eggs
and hid them in the garden for her to find; when
she did find them her mother would embrace her
wildly and plant kisses like one possessed. She
sighed. Paused her prayer. Memories darkened.
Francis kissed also, but his kisses were from lust
not love as he had claimed during the all too
frequent copulations. She kissed the small
crucifix. The small Crucified on the rosary, silver
and twisted, seemed to shiver in the cold of the
church. Pray for us now and at the hour of our
death, she muttered, brushing the beads against
her cheek. Her sister Margaret stiff and cold in
her cot found by her mother. No one told her
until the coffin came. *Poor Margaret. Poor baby.*
Her cries at night smothered by blankets so some

had said. The tide of her mother's madness ebbed and flowed until it flooded her mind; drowned her mother's sweetness in the dark hell of her fears and ghosts. Sister Gabrielle entered the church; sat beside her; her arm touched her own; her whispered words soft as flower petals seeped into her ears. *Are you there, Mother?* Long silences; all too long the silences between words. Her mother's lucidity rare and infrequent; her mother's caresses stiff and oddly indifferent. Sister, be near, now and at the hour. Sighed. The Crucified's limbs were taut; His lips sealed; His hands pierced, curved in agony. Sunlight seeped through the high windows; the nun beside her caught the sun's soft rays in her open hands; the fingers held a black rosary studded with rubies like the bl*ood of Christ. F*rancis had never loved her; his lust lingered in her mind like a sore. Some days she hid in a cupboard to hide from her father's rage; his hitting hand hard on her soft flesh. Forgive them for they know not, the words seeped through her lips. *Glory be to the sun and the sunlight on the sister's hands* and the rosary held between finger and thumb. *Pray for us. Your kingdom com*e. Mother's last gaze distant and aloof; her final words disjointed, floating on the air on that last visit before her sudden death. The tomb is empty. He has gone. Her father's faith slipped through his fingers like sand; his eyes, dark and cruel, resurrected themselves in her memory as she muttered over the final bead's prayer. *I have lifted my eyes*, she whispered, *to the hig*h windows, to catch the light and flood out the darkness of my days and nights. Sighed. Closed her eyes. Peace. Come. Peace. Peace.

Easter Sunday.

Sister Scholastica passed the salt to the nun beside her on the refectory table. Anticipation of the needs of others; charity in action; the nun nodded and smiled. The roast beef succulent; the dark-brown gravy and mouth-watering Yorkshire pudding part of the celebration of the Crucified's resurrection. She cut slowly through the meat, her eyes lifted toward the nun reading opposite from the Rule of St Benedict, her ears capturing the stiff voice of Sister Mary. Mother, before her mind dissolved into madness, made Sunday her blessed day with her roasts; the pork done to a turn, as Father used to say when his temper was even; his smacking hand at rest. Her mother's eyes were bright, but showed the beginnings of the madness creeping; her father laughed too infrequently at the joys of life then. She sipped at the red wine; held the glass close to her lips to sip again. Warming. You go to my head. Wine always did. Francis, whom she nearly married, poured her wine until she was pliable; they copulated in her parent's bed when they were off for the weekend on a business venture of her father's. She sipped; felt the inner glow. The tomb was empty, the body gone. The Crucified had risen. Francis rose up when he heard a car pull up in the driveway; panic when her parents returned early. Rush. Tidied up the bed. Sighed. The wine is good. The beef held in the mouth to take in the juices. *Este es el día de Cristo elevadose*, Sister Mary had said to her after mass, touching her hand, smiling, maybe wanting more, the day *Christ is raised*, she said in English, her eyes sparkling like a cut diamond in sunlight. Sister Gabrielle passed her more potatoes; charity in action; remembering others. *We are unimportant,* her mother had said, *the cross symbolizes the negation of self, the I crossed out.* Selfless, her mother's voice repeated on her lucid days sandwiched between madness and light. She lifted her eyes to the high windows; saw the sunlight play on the head of the nun reading, dance across the floor of the refecto*ry.* Would the sister pass more wine? Who knows. Charity in action. Mother drank gin and when she'd drunk herself merry would dance with me around the lounge much to Father's annoyance and he grumbled and moaned. The nun on her left passed the wine. Refilled her glass. Smiled. Father rarely smiled. Never, once Mother was in the asylum and her baby sister Margaret buried in the small white coffin. *Christ is raised; Christ will come once more. Father forgive me, I didn't know your heart was so cold,* she wanted to say to him, but never did, especially after he beat her and left her in the cold dark room where her sister had died in her cot. The wine warmed. She gazed at the Crucified on the cross above the Abbess's table, His arms out wide as if to embrace the sinful world, inside and outside of the cloister. The crown of thorns hammered into the skull uncomfortably. Risen. The tomb empty. The body gone. Her mother, father, sister and Francis had gone. No resurrection of them except in her memory and the haunting dreams. Easter Sunday. The wine, the blood of Christ, saved. She sighed. Gazed over at Sister Mary, whose eyes moved over the page as she read, and felt charity inwardly, remembered the touch, the hand warm, the voice near her ear speaking the Spanish of her childhood saying: *Amor en acción, love in action.* Sisters. Saved. *Blessed is He who rose.*

Lighten my darkness. Save me from my ghosts and memories. Amen.

SISTER AGNES'S DAWN.

I rise with the morning bell, said Sister Agnes, *I hear it now in my ears. It rings in the ears and heart. The window shows dawn just about to come over the cloister wall like a mischievous child about to play forbidden games. I sing in choir with my voice absorbed by the voices of others and the walls of the church. I walk the cell like one waiting to die; listen to the birdsong outside like one wanting new life or life renewed. Sister Blaise is in the cloister garth walking with the birds, the morning chill resting on her black serge shoulder. I watch her walk; her feet tread like one on eggshells. Her hands hidden beneath her blackbird breast, her head bowed like one at prayer. She has birds at her feet, St Francis like. I shall leave her, kneel in prayer, and climb the stairway to contemplation. My father's tears settle on my sight; his voice broken; his eyes looking out at the garden where once we walked. He would have had me stay at home; dry old-maid fashion at his beck and call day and night as my mother did until cancer dragged her weeping to the far beyond. I shut my lids against the dawn; press my lids like one seeking blindness to the harsh day's light. My brother, George, sits in some Paris café talking of art and painting his oil-drench canvases in his back street studio. Father talks of him as one who is lost. Both of us are lost to him, each in their own way. George cares not; his art and women are his all. Thoughts push their way through the curtains of my prayer; they are rude and unclean; they are ill-bred like the children my mother despised. I rise from prayer like one defeated. The light from the dawn blesses me with warmth; my flesh touched like one in love. I look at Sister Blaise and her birds; her hands are open like one crucified. Her rosary hangs from her belt; a thousand prayers cling to each bead. Last night I saw her kiss the feet of the stone Virgin; lay her hand on the Saviour's head. Holiness nests in her heart like a white bird in a dark bush; she shall hold me in my dim hours. The bell rings once more; its echo vibrates my ears and heart. I was happy when I entered Your house; Your handmaiden shall attend Your needs. Prayers escape me; liturgies are my food and drink; my beads shall be my stones of pain. My aches shall be the nails to crucify me in my dark hours; my Christ bleeds in my monthly* death. All shall be forgiven. The stones shall break my bones; the words pierce my fleshy heart. I shall go now; descend the stairs for dawn time prayer. Night flees me like one unfaithful to a lover's kiss. I come. My bridegroom.

HERE COMES THE BRIDE.

I love the birds and the song of birds, said Sister Blaise. *I hear the voice of my bridegroom when they sing; in the flapping of their wings; when they peck at my hands I feel His presence. The cloister garth's flowers have His scent about them; the breeze speaks to me of Him, how unworthy I am to be His bride. Sister Agnes peers at me from her window; I pretend not to see or to know. Her eyes are always upon me; she seeks me out like one wanting company. In the cloister at night after Compline, she wanders in my shadow as I make my way to my cell for prayer and sleep. I am the unworthy bride; I chastise my flesh for my ways and sins. My sister, Charlotte, bathes in her sins like one preparing for a party, and as a child, she would pull wings off butterflies; throw frogs in the air awaiting them to fly. She says I am wasting my life on a crucified lie; that my womb will stink of death. I*

touch the feet of my bridegroom's mother; she
smiles at my words and simple gaze. My mother
spoke of my bridegroom with jealousy; her words
echo in my mind across the years. Unworthy to
be His, she said, unworthy to be at His side, she
muttered, as I knelt in prayer or rubbed my
beads. I love the dawn; the light that comes like
my bridegroom to wake me from slumber. He is
handsome; my heart leaps when He takes my
hand and leads me to my work and prayer. At
night, I embrace Him; listen to His words in the
wind that rattles my window. David embraced me
once; kissed me on our way home from the
cinema. He spoke of marriage; the outpouring of
children; the ways of the flesh. His hand was
upon me; his lips brushed against mine. Now he
has married another; she is barren as an empty
barrel; freezes when he touches her with his
pinkie pores. The bell rings for Lauds. My
bridegroom waits for my voice and praise; He
sits in His chamber for my attendance and words
to flow over Him like water. Sister Elizabeth
walks with her eyes lowered; her hands are
joined in her secret prayer; she knows my
bridegroom like my matron-of-honour; she kisses
my cheek in the dreams of her night. In the
refectory she stares at me from across the room;
her hands held in front gesturing words. My
bridegroom awaits; His attendants prepare His

robes of white and red; His bride enters His chamber with a smile and her love. I want Him to come to me, His hand to touch my brow and embrace my flesh. The perfume of His incense enfolds me; His voice speaks of my secret love; my heart leaps when He touches my tongue. I sing to Him; wrap my words to the music of voices; kneel before Him like one making love in the raptures of feelings, prayers and the morning's cold kiss. I have come, my love, I am here for your blessing and kisses.

SISTER ELIZABETH'S MORNING SONG.

I watch the rain pour into the cloister garth, said Sister Elizabeth. *It batters the flowers into sad submission. The cloister is my shelter from the rain and the wickedness of the world. I used to watch the downpour of the rain from the nursery window as a child; Molly, the maid, said rain was the tears of God for the woes of the world. I saw the raindrops hit against the pane and tried to touch them with my fingers. Sister Blaise kissed the Madonna in the cloister last night; she closed her eyes like one in love. She is my sister*

*in Christ, my love of heart and head. I watch her
in my secret way; her bridegroom is my
bridegroom, too. My sister, Vivien, visits me in
my lonely hours; she was my one companion. She
married the Monster of Manchester who beats
her and neglects her wants and needs. The
raindrops hit the flower heads, the flowers bend
and flop like beaten wives. My father dreamed of
better things; my mother painted in the attic; her
paintings hang in their frames like the captured
dead. Sister Blaise comes through the cloister;
her walk inflames my heart and head. She kneels
by the statue of Christ and kisses His feet; her
lips brush the tortured one. She must not see me
gazing; I must look away like a child seeing its
parents kiss. Father kissed my mother as she
painted hell; the colours haunt my nights with the
screams she painted. Sister Blaise walks behind
me; her feet tread her own Golgotha. In the
refectory I watch her hands as they rise and fall;
I watch her face as she listens; her lips as she
eats and prays. The bell from the tower rings for
Terce; I must leave the rain and battered flowers
and enter the church. The wind in the cloister
whispers about me; the wind, said Molly, is the
whispering of God. Il dio è il miei amore e guida,
Sister Francis says; God is my love and guides
me; my bridegroom awaits me; my bridegroom
wants my presence in His chamber. My fingers*

dip in the stoup; the water cleanses my hands
like Pilate before me. The sisters are gathered;
the abbess stares at the hanging Christ, fingering
her beads like a child at play. My mother's art
haunts my nights; the colours torment like
Dante's Inferno. Sister Blaise is near to my side;
her voice is close to my ear. Molly whispered
words to help me sleep; her arms enfolded me in
my childhood fears; her warm breath tickled my
neck in my hours of sleep. Sister Francis stands
opposite; her eyes lowered like a self-conscious
bride, her hands caressing the breviary like a
babe in arms. In my heart and soul, my
bridegroom murmurs; His whispering voice
echoes around me; His closeness comes and goes
like waves of the sea. Last night I dreamed of
Sister Blaise; her lips and mine met in a holy
kiss; her hand and mine touched like doves in
proximity. The smell of incense lingers nearby;
the scent of Sister Blaise mingles and soothes. I
read and sing; my voice lost in the voices of
others, my soul awaiting my loving groom.
Father drank in his secret room; he lost his God
in the battles of war. His friends' deaths haunted
his dreams; his soul was starved of all grace and
light. My bridegroom hangs from His cross all
battered and torn; His limbs are spread wide to
embrace the world as He embraces me in my
nights of climbing to prayer. The voices are still;

the office is ended. We rise and go like brides to our labours; like brides we walk with minds on our bridegroom; set to our tasks like ones in love. I come, my precious; my warm hands are ready; my lips await your abundant kisses.

SISTER FRANCIS AND HER MIDDAY HOUR.

He has pierced my side with His lance of love, said Sister Francis, *He counts my bones with His holy hands. None sees my wound; none knows of my constant pain. The cloister is my Golgotha, the walls my Jerusalem where I walk with my sisters. The clock chimes like the voice of God, the hours and minutes His to command. My brother Nigel kissed me once in our childhood games; his hands explored my girlhood like a gallant knight, his eyes looking with those of a hawk. Sleepless nights often remind me; his gaze haunts my nightly dreams with the power of sin. My father counted money with the coldness of ice; his fingers were green with the coins of the realm. He embraced us only when drink had engulfed him, loved us less than the favour of money; his look was icy as the frozen north. Sister Thomas walks by the statue of Christ; her fingers touch with the gentlest of touches. She stops and looks; her eyes have the colour of a summer's sky; her hands as soft as the finest of silk. I remember the touch when she felt my temple, when I fainted in the church one hot summer's day. She walks to the wall of the garth and the garden; her nose smells the flowers like seeking a lover; her fingers embrace a stem as fond lovers do. My mother's mind was fickle and fragile; her eyes were too tearful; she wandered about in her own private world; spoke of the angels at the foot of her bed. I see the birds that sing at my window, I love their songs that open my day. The thrush and the blue tit are my constant companions; their presence and friendship are the joy of my life. I walk to the garth and wonder in silence; watch as birds move round in their dance. Nigel and I once kissed in the forest; his lips and mine like Guinevere and Arthur, sometimes his Lancelot would seek and explore. Mother cringed like a beaten child; her eyes lowered to the carpeted floor. She embraced me once like one who is dying; her hands felt like ice when her fingers touched. Sister Thomas speaks, but her words are too quiet, I cannot discover the message she gives. I saw her last night as she walked in the*

*cloister; I wanted her closer to whisper and hold
me, wanted her words to embrace and to kiss.
Dio è il miei amore e guida, I say in my mind's
private language, God is my love and guides me
through passages to my crucifixion, His hand
touching mine through the coldest of nights. The
bell rings for Sext the hour of prayer; I turn to go
from the birds and the bees, my feet treading the
paths to prayer and song. Sister Thomas follows;
her footsteps beside me; she moves so close our
shadows embrace. The sisters come like sheep to
the slaughter; each with their sorrows and sins to
the Bridegroom, His love and mercy their one
holy passion; His touch and kiss their nightly
haunt. We enter the church, a companion of
sisters; our oneness and bride-ship the mark of
our bridegroom, His presence so near unites us
in bond-ship, His scent and whispers our
constant reminder; our sins and aloneness He
knows us too well. My mother's knees were sore
where she knelt too often; her hands were red
where she washed them too much. Father's cold
touch never embraced her; his words were
colder than ice in the winter, his eyes as dark as
the night of his moods. We settle in our places;
the choir begins. The voices of angels, my mother
said when she visited me once in my novice trial
years, her fingers all fidget, her hands held each
other in nervous embracing. Come my*

bridegroom, empty my mind of the things of the past; embrace me and kiss me, Your lover and bride. My crucifixion is in my nightly sweats; Your loving gaze pierces my side; my heart is blessed by Your care and compassion; my soul hungers for Your light and love when the darkness comes and my flesh is so weak. Come my bridegroom, your bride awaits; her flesh all-a tingle, her heart wide open as the door to her soul.

Requiem.

Mother Josephine dead. It's hard to believe, Sister Teresa muses to herself as she leaves the church after Sext. *So long ago now since I first saw her. Thirty years ago, yes, thirty years ago.* And as she walks along the cloister towards the refectory, she thinks over the many years of their relationship. The sun shines into the cloister and warms the ground beneath her feet. She passes the bell rope hanging like a tail in the cloister outside the refectory door. *It was here*, she says to herself as she enters the refectory, *it was here that Mother Josephine first spoke to me all those years ago.* And entering the refectory she bows towards the crucifix on the wall above Mother Abbess's table and goes to the old table where the bread is laid out for the sisters. She cuts herself two slices of brown bread and takes her place at the table where she has sat for the last six months. *Yes, here,* she repeats to herself, *it was here that Mother Josephine first spoke to me that late evening that I arrived on my first visit to the convent.* She stands by the table and awaits the arrival of Mother Abbess through the door. *It seems years now since that evening. Thirty years. God. How time has flown.* And seeing Mother Abbess enter, Sister Teresa bows towards her and waits for the signal to begin the grace. Tap tap and the grace begins and she recites the grace that she has said so many times now, that it seems like an eternity since she first said it way back in 1968. *That long ago? Yes, I suppose it is,* she thinks, sitting down at her place as the grace ends. *And Mother Josephine was even then like a mother hen towards me that late evening I arrived. What did I ask her? Hard to recall now. Something about what qualifications I might need to enter the community, I think. And Mother Josephine said, returning from the kitchen where she had been to fetch me some warm food, only your willingness to serve and love of Go*d. *And I felt her wanting me to be there so much.* Sister

Teresa waits for the food to be brought to the table by one of the younger nuns. She looks across at the table opposite and sees Sister Martha pick up a glass and fill it with water from a glass jug on the table. *So many have left or died over the years,* she sighs looking away from Sister Martha. She waits until one of the young ones places a tray of meat and vegetables on the table and then offers it to her sisters on the right and left of her. They help themselves and then she, indifferently, takes a portion of each on to her plate and begins to eat. *Mother Josephine has died*, Mother Abbess had said that morning after mass in the chapter house. And the community had not been that surprised, but it had shocked Sister Teresa. *It seemed as if old Mother Josephine would last forever, but of course she didn't. Silly to think she would. Not think so much as wished it probably*, she muses eating a portion and looking at the window up above her opposite. *And Lucia not long gone either. It seems so many have gone recently. Lucia so suddenly last year. Shocked me that did and pained me terribly*, she muses darkly putting down her fork and pushing food around the plate. *Mother Josephine dead. Just like that. No more to know her about the house as such. No more to see her enter the church for Lauds or Vespers and Mass as she did those final weeks with effort.*

I wonder if she ever knew about Lucia and me. She may I think. When Lucia went to Rome way back in 1971 and I had problems settling down she had me sent home for a few weeks to recover. Breakdown of sorts. But she knew about us I'm sure. She said nothing, but knew. Kind and gentle. Different from some that were here. Sister Teresa sips from the glass of water in front of her and gazes across at Sister Maria who is eating slowly from her plate. And then she looks up towards Mother Abbess who waits for the reader to finish the given text of the day. She cleans her knife, fork and spoon with her napkins and puts it away beneath the table ready for the next meal. *Mother Abbess has finally settled dow*n, Sister Teresa muses to herself. *So sudden after Lucia's death. And Mother Josephine was always there then to guide the new Abbess.* The tap tap from the Abbess and the reader stops in mid-sentence. All rise and the grace after the meal begins. After the Abbess has departed, the other nuns depart in whatever fashion and Sister Teresa walks out from the refectory and along the cloister in the sunshine. S*o alone now,* Sister Teresa thinks, *since Lucia went. Now even more so. The young are unfamiliar. The old too locked in their own world. Thirty years since I entered,* she says to herself, as she walks along the cloister looking into the garth surrounded by flowers. And she remembers the time Mother Josephine came to the common room when she stayed that time in 1968 and said, *Mother Abbess says you can enter in the autumn.* But in fact she had entered in December because of other commitments and hence the late evening arrival, she thinks walking down the steps that lead into the grounds. *Cold that year. Never known it so. But it was all part of the sacrifice I thought then,* she tells herself as she walks slowly down the path leading to the beach. *Now I take things in my stride*, she muses smiling to herself and letting the sunshine warm her face. *Never used to walk alone so much as I do now*, she sighs, placing her hands inside her habit, *there were usually others to walk with: Martha, Lucia, and of course Mother Josephine. Sometimes Martha comes and we walk along here, but it's not the same. Years have given us little to talk about apart from the rumours and gossip. Mother Josephine is eighty-seven you know; Martha had said a few weeks back, I remember,* Sister Teresa informs herself. *Been a professed nun for seventy years. That's some time, Martha had added as we conversed along the cloister during our recreation period. Seventy years. I thought my thirty years was good*, Sister Teresa muses. She looks up at the bright warm sunlight filtering through the trees above her head. She stands still for a few minutes and looks up and then around her. *We used to walk here during our recreation with Mother Josephine those early years as novices. Georgina, Geraldine, Young Sister Henry and I. Never did quite take to Sister Henry. Gone now. Left years ago and married. Georgina and Geraldine left also after a year or so. Many called, few chosen, so the saying goes. And Mother would take us along here and down onto the private beach. We never sunbathed of course or anything like that. Just sat on the beach and watched the tide come in and out and talked and talked and occasionally in our youthfulness threw stones along the water. And Mother would join in too. So long ago*, Sister Teresa says just above a whisper, *so long ago*. And she walks down on to the beach and stands looking out to sea. *Sometimes Sister Lucy and I would come down here and just stand here. Sometimes we would hold hands and walk along the whole private stretch of beach. Once we saw Mother and quickly dropped our hands. She may have seen us, but she never said or mentioned it. She never even tried to keep us apart as some may have done had they seen us so much together. But she never did. I can see her no*w standing here, her warm friendly eyes through narrow-wired glasses looking at me. Sister Teresa walks along the beach and hides her hands in her habit. She feels the salt from the sea on her tongue and in her nose. She closes her eyes and stands still again. *Only the sound of the waves and the cry of far off seagulls now. I remember that time I went to see her because I had a falling out with Sister Henry. Yes, even here one can have falling outs, though one tries to resolve things not let them fester or become difficult. That is part of the test, Teresa. We all have our funny ways that may annoy another. We are all human. We may find others not to our taste or not those whom we would choose as friends. But we are bound by our vows and love of Christ to see Christ in all our sisters not just those whom we like or love, Mother had said. She may have been hinting about Lucy and me, but she never said anything about names or such. Try to make an effort to see Christ especially in Sister Henry, Mother added looking at me through her glasses. I said I'd try. I did try and it made a difference. But we never really liked each other deep down, Sister Henry and I. Don't know why. Strange. But can you love someone whom you don't like? Possibly. I mean you may not always like those whom you love, but you love them all the same. And others you like, but not necessarily love. Well so I thought. Now I'm not sure. Mother was wise. She, who had been a nun for seventy years, knew human nature better than* I. Sister Teresa opens her eyes again and looks out to sea. *Sometimes, I remember, Sister James would come along on our walks. She was our assistant novice-mistress. I liked her. She had a great sense of humour and could throw stones along the waves better than any of us way back then. She too has left now. Mother Josephine was indeed like a mother hen to us who came into her care. Once she had retired, she was allowed to take things easy, but she rarely did. She hated to be unoccupied. I bet even now she's asking Our Lord for things to do. People to pray for. Rest in peace, Mother,* Sister Teresa says over the incoming tide. *Now a bell rings. Recreation is over. Better return to the house,* she says to herself as she turns back along the beach. And as she enters the cloister she senses that maybe Mother isn't far away. Just there. Watching. Listening. Smiling.

EASTER 1971.

My baby brother died on Easter Day, says Sister Elizabeth, *his arms outstretched stiff in his cot like some miniature Christ. My mother found him and it broke her heart; she clutched him tightly to her breast as if life might return; she had to be sedated to unlatch her hold, the baby still stiff and cold. Sister Peter rings the bell; the sisters flow silently along the cloister; the spring flowers unfold like children at play. I hold my mother's image in my mind, her final days before her jump to her death from the bridge, that last look in her eyes I carry with me as I walk the cloister with the sunlight's blessing upon robes. My father left unable to cope with my mother's moods, swings, and dark days; he writes from his studio in Turin, his artist fingers mark the page. The statue of Our Lady is decked with flowers; prayers on paper are tucked beneath her feet; she stares out at the blue morning sky. I place my fingers in the stoup and feel the cold water touch the tips; I mark a cross from head to breast from shoulder to shoulder and take my place in the choir stalls, the light from high windows spread upon the flagstone floor like spilt gold. The Crucified hangs over the altar; His arms outstretched like my baby brother; His eyes are closed as if in sleep; His love keeps close in my night of soul. The sisters filter into chapel and take their places; Sister Bede gives me her smile that would warm in winter; the tiny hands clutch the breviary, the red-ended pages contrast with the white of the page. I smell the incense from mass; it lingers around me like a lover's hold. My father painted Christ on the wall of his room; his Christ has no eyes, just shapes like tears and a mouth forming an O with dark skin and robes like snow. My mother's tears almost drowned me in my youth; her wounding words battered my skin; her closed heart kept me away, would not let me in. The Easter chant touches the roof and walls of the chapel; the voices rising and falling like waves of the sea; a unison of praise reaching for God, each word a parcel and gift, a hope, a prayer. The chanting is over; the sisters file out into the morning sun; I sense its warmth on head and skin and lift my face to the light like one waiting to be kissed. My mother's ghost wanders at my side; her arms hold her phantom child; her eyes are bright like new minted coins laid in the sun. I wait by the wall of the cloister garth and sense my mother's words flutter about me like startled birds; her ghostly hand reaches for mine to make up lost time, while clutching her baby against her breast with her vacant hand, the fingers holding the head like some Stabat Mater with her lifeless son.*

Waiting and Serving.

Sister Bede stirs the soup simmering on the
stove. The steam rises upwards like incense. She
can hear her mother saying, *you got a degree to
stir soup? Three years at Oxford to waste away
in some convent with a honours degree, stirring
soup?* She can hear her mother's words cackling
like hens. Beef soup, thick and hot. She watches
it go around in the huge saucepan. Clockwise
then anticlockwise. Slowly stirring. M*other
never wanted me to be a nun,* she mutters to
herself, looking over her shoulder at Sister
Frances cutting the meat, her eyes focused, her
hands busy. Her mother had threatened to cut her
off, but she never did, she always had to have a
dig, always say things about the nuns and her
favourite saying was, *shutting yourself away with
all those queer old women.* They're not all old.
Some are my age, some younger. She looks back
at the soup. She pauses stirring. *Nearly read*y.
She spoons out a small drop and tastes. *Just
right.* She puts the spoon in the sink. Sister
Frances brings the trolley with meat, vegetables,
gravy and helps Sister Bede lift the huge
saucepan on to the trolley and pours some soup
into smaller tureens. Not a word is exchanged;
just gestures with hands and fingers and facial

expressions. *Ready*. She pushes the trolley into the refectory; the nuns are all there. Waiting. *The abbess is at the far end waiting, her eyes downcast in prayer or deep thought*, Sister Bede muses, pushing the trolley to where Sister Joseph waits ready to help serve. Mother would find this so inexplicable. A room of women standing, waiting in silence. Her scornful voice ghostly echoes in her ears. She stands and waits. Sister Leo stands to her left. She tries not to gaze too obviously. So tall. So elegant. The robes make her look so saintly. Sister Leo smiles discreetly. Flutter. Her heart flutters. Sister Bede looks away; pretends to be busy, shifting spoons quietly. She's still looking. Smiling still. Her eyes dark as rooks; her lips open just enough to allow air in. The hands crossed, slim fingers touching. Sister Bede hears the tap and nod from the abbess. Time to begin. The nun on the platform begins to read from a book. All others are silent waiting for food and water. She lifts the tureen of soup on to the nearest table and places a large ladle beside it. She looks up and Sister Leo is busy pouring water for a nun next door to her. Thoughtful. Charitable. Sister Bede carries another tureen of soup to the next table, knowing eyes were on her now. Sister Leo watches as she passes by. Flutter. The heart catches in her breast. She moves on to the next table and lifts the tureen on to the top. She waits now. Stands still; eyes downwards. She catches the odd phrases from the nun reading. Not the word of God; some book on Cromwell, she believes. Her mother would shake her head at this standing around. *What a waste. Time waits for no one*, she often said. *Time is no one's servant.* Lifting her eyes she gazes at Sister Leo spooning soup slowly to her lips. Those lips. Soft spoken. Words flow from them like a Mozartian melody. There was that kiss. Kisses. She puts the thoughts away. Tries to catch more words from the nun reading, pushes the images from her mind, sees sunlight make a straight piercing ray of light onto the refectory floor. Warmth. A trickle of perspiration runs down her spine. She wants to mop her brow; senses beads of sweat clinging there. Such a waste Mother would say, all those old queer women thrown together behind high walls. She pushes her mother's words away; lift her eyes to the crucifix above the abbess's table, the Christ staring down, the dark eyes searching, the arms outstretched, beads of sweat and blood hang on His brow. *Love is all there is to know; she knows that now.*

Awaiting Lunch

Sister Charles tucks in the large white napkin into the neck of her black habit and gazes around the refectory. Odd seeing so many other women gathered and such silence. No tongues wagging; no gossip. Only the nun reading, up on the platform above the tables, drones on over the silence. There is only the knocking of water jugs and glasses and moving of chairs, she reminds herself, looking through her thick lenses. She lifts the spoon and gazes at her reflection in the back. Distorted her image stares back at her. She and her sister did that as children. She recalls sticking out her tongue and her father scolding her for bad manners at the table at home. She rubs the spoon with the napkin. She feels she wants to wash the spoon rather than lick it clean as they do after meals and place it with the knife and fork in the huge napkin and push it under her place at the table in the refectory. Father would not have liked that at all. Once a week all cutlery is steamed in the kitchen and clean ones handed out to start all over again. So one doesn't get too possessive of property, she assumes putting the spoon down on the table top. She looks up to see which of the nuns are serving. Sister Joseph with her large white apron over her habit pushes the food trolley into the center of the refectory. Sister

Bede stands beside it gazing at the abbess's top table waiting for the nod from the abbess for the meal to begin. She saw Sister Bede once coming out of the shower with ginger hair of a few inches all over her head. Strange seeing another nun without her headdress on. When she first came and realized they were only permitted a bath or shower once a week she felt so unclean after a few days she imagined herself smelling. The luxury of a daily bath or shower is long gone now, she tells herself looking toward the abbess's table, waiting for the nod of head. Her stomach rumbles gently. She waits for her glass to be filled by an obliging sister. It stands there empty. *Nuns must not help themselves, but await the charity of a sister.* She looks around her hoping Sister Peter will oblige. Sister Peter sits with eyes closed. At prayer or tired, she assumes, looking at Sister James on the other side who smiles and lifts the water jug and pours water into the glass. Sister Charles smiles a thank you and pours water into the nun's own glass. She sips the water; cold and clear. She runs it around her mouth with her tongue and then swallows it. Lovely. She needed it that. She holds the glass close to her lips and sips again. Never gulp, mother had said years ago, it so unladylike. She allows the water to slowly run over and over her tongue until she swallows it down. The abbess nods and taps on her table and the meal begins. The serving nuns start to serve up the portion for each table. *There is a humbleness in their movement; any sense of the task being below them has long since been pushed away. Serve your sisters as if it was Christ Himself you serve; Him you wait on and provide for and serve,* Sister of Novices had told her years before. Again her stomach rumbles. Soon be coming. The meal. Soup. Hot and beefy. The nun on her left pours ladlefuls of soup into Sister Charles's large white bowl and then her own and passes the soup tureen along the table to the nun on Sister Charle's left. Sister Charles pours ladlefuls of soup into white bowl of the nun on her left and then lifts her spoon and just before she dips it in the soup she sees her reflected distorted image looking back her and smiles. She dips in the spoon and lifts the spoonful of soup to her lips and feels the warmness flow into her mouth and the rumbling stomach is silenced as she swallows and senses the warmness seep into her. Funny the silence of these women. Only the nun reading makes a sound; her voice drones on over the silence like a bee over summer flowers.

Cramps & Prayers.

Sister Leo kneels by her bed in her room. Conversations, prayers, whatever, her father said, waste of time, best get out in the real world and put your shoulder to the wheel. She remembers his words like beestings. God was an anathema to him; his arch-enemy if he ever thought He existed at all. She feels an ache in her knees; her thighs feel crampy. She closes her eyes. Breathes in deep. Keep those old thoughts out. Mother was too timid; said nothing when Father bellowed, when he hit her, when he dragged her from her knees half in prayer to scrub the floor in the downstairs' toilet after Mother'd defecated with the cancer and all. She brings her hands together; feels the flesh on flesh. Warm. Rubs them; feels the friction. Lifting her mind and heart. The Crucified on the wall above her bed. She opens her eyes and looks up. Framed picture. Often gazes at Him. Speaks, utters prayers. Above her pillow, a plain wooden cross. The symbol of torture; of negation; of salvation. Old wood; time stained. Sister James had said, *It's the I crossed out, the negation of self. Lost in darkness. No light some days. But he's there*, Sister James had insisted. *Always there.* She closes the eyes again. Holds the breath. Did that as a child to see how long she could hold it. Or maybe a way to die. Out of it all back then. Father as he was; *Mother dying of cancer. Thin as a reed in the end. Blown by ill winds. Where's your God now?* Father'd say. *Where the great almighty right now?* He bellowed staring her right in the face, his huge brown eyes boring into her. *Forgive those that interfere with us,* she mutters, thinking of her father, *not wanting to, wanting him long gone.* Even in the convent within its high walls, he's there in her memory, ghostly walking the cloisters, mocking, taunting. *Without forgiveness there can be no forgiveness, without remorse no mercy, no pardon.* She allows prayers to rise, fresh prayers, new ones. Her knees ache still. The thighs have cramp. She rises awkwardly and paces the room, rubbing the back of her thighs with her hands. Sister Bede gazed at her lunchtime. *The eyes bright as stars. The smile warm as an embrace. Not to dwell on that. Not to lose focus. Whatever you focus on is your reality*, Father had insisted. *All things are just atoms in motion; no reality you can see. You can stick your God, child, no way that's a reality.* She had wanted to tell him he was wrong, but she feared him. The dark eyes brooded; the large hands smacked. She squeezes her eyes shut tight trying to keep him out and God in. She pauses and stands by the window looking down into the cloister. Sister Bede is pulling weeds in the garth flowerbeds. The fingers busy; the back bent. She watches the scene for several minutes taking in each motion, each movement, each pause for rest. God is in each part of us inward dwelling. Never found Him in her father no mattered how hard she looked. But Sister Bede…she sighs. The cramp in her thighs has eased. Offer it up, the pain, the prayer, the thoughts, the wants, the sins, the deeds, the kisses. He sees all; there's nothing He misses.

Her Mother said.

The rosary feels light between her fingers. Sister James rubs the black wooden beads as if a thousands prayers could be brought back into being. Smooth. The touch of the thumb rubbing over the beads. Many Aves and Pater Nosters have been worked in here she muses lifting her eyes to the light coming through the window. The sunlight makes patterns on the wooden floorboards. The smell of flowers filters in from the open window; sounds of birdsong are all she can hear. She closes her eyes. If *I had a penny for each prayer I'd be a millionair*e she muses, sniffing the room, sensing the polish, the soap scrubbed hands, the starch in the black habit. She can feel the hard floor beneath her knees. She moves them. Brings them touching. Knee on knee side by side. She sits on her heels. Rests there. Mother had taught her how to pray. Hours on hour as a little girl sitting on her heels, repeating the prayers her mother taught, a slap on the hand if she got it wrong. Mother would carry her rosary around with her tucked in the belt around her waist. It would hang there, dark brown and heavy, the Crucified going back and forth as she walked. Sister James opens her eyes, gets up, and rubs her knees with her right hand. The rosary hangs from her left, the Christ well rubbed, shines in the sunlight. She walks to the window and peers out into the cloister garth. Sister Bede is weeding the flowerbeds. Sunlight blesses her head. Her hands move amongst flowers, dragging out weeds and pushing them into a pile by her legs. Mother could say the Pater Noster so fast it seemed like a spell. Her mother's dark eyes peered across at her if she made mistake or uttered a wrong word in the prayers or readings from the Bible. A smack on the back of her leg with a wet hand stung for ages after. *Making mistakes in prayers shows the Devil's at work,* she'd say. Sister James watches as Sister Bede rubs her hands to removed damp soil. She wipes her brow. Slight sweat clinging. She sits back on her heels and looks at the sky.

Birds fly near by. The mulberry tree is full of fruit. Teatime on hot days the sisters have their afternoon tea in the cloister garth, gathering around the trolley with cups and saucers and slices of cake and biscuits and chattering briefly before the bell tolled again. Mother's hands were cold and thin. When she held the hand or slapped the leg, they warmed. *Always remember your prayers*, Mother said. *Beware of young men and their thoughts and deeds and do not allow them to touch.* Since Father had left she knew nothing of men, knew nothing of their ways or thoughts or deeds and only Edward had touched her once briefly after mass and her mother never saw so that didn't count. She leans forward out of the window and sees Sister Leo at her window looking out at Sister Bede. An audience. Two sisters peering at one weeding. She steps away from the window and walks to the bed and peers at the Christ hanging from the huge cross on the wall. Not a speck of dust there. Not a sign of spider's webs or dirt. Mother had one like this in her room hanging above her bed. Cobwebs hung there; dust and dirt. The Crucified peering out with heavy eyes. Mother sometimes dragged her there and forced her to kneel. *Tell the Lord what* you've done, *go on tell Him all your sins, relate to your Saviour how you deserve Hell*, Mother would yell, gripping the arm, bending down the head. Sister James reaches out and touches the crown of thorns, the nails seem so real. No dust or dirt. She rubs the thorns. Mother related the five wounds: the crown of thorns, the nails in hand and feet and the wound in His side. *See*, Mother would say, *there look, and she'd take the small hand and trust it into the slit made in the plaster Christ. Each time you are bad and sin, you push the nails and thorns in deepe*r, Mother would bellow, holding the small finger and pushing it on to the nails in hands and feet of the Christ. Once the finger bled where she'd pushed so hard. Sister James rubs the nails in hands and feet of the Christ on the crucifix on the wall. She hasn't seen her mother since her last visit to the asylum seven years before. Never spoke; just stared and muttered and rubbed at a rosary between her thin fingers. Dark rings around her eyes through lack of sleep. Sister James kisses her fingertips and places the kiss on the five wounds of Christ. *His bride loves Him. She loves as He loves, not to be loved, but to love, even if love is not returned, even if the object of that love seems so unlovable, love must still love, and that is the love she loves her mother with, the love without strings or conditions or limitations a*nd as she smiles at her Christ she recalls her mother's last hard stare as she left her there at the asylum with a staleness in the air and her mother's prayer like distant unforgiving hum.

Sister Luke's Lent.

You withdraw the rosary from your inner pocket
and hold it in your hand and gaze at it taking in
the cross with the Christ in black ebony and the
way He lies there in your hand His eyes closed
and His arms out stretched and His hands
screwed up into almost a fist but not so just
expressing an agony and you remember as a
child your father taking your hand and stubbing a
cigarette there deep until your screams unsettled
your mother from her drugged sleep but she said
nothing but slept on and the rosary sits there now
and the light from the church window shines on
your hand and the rosary and you sigh for the
inner joy of that and the dark memory of your
father's hand on your thigh at night when he crept
in your room and sat by your bed and stroked
you and whispered all kinds of words and let his
fingers walk to places your mother said were
your sacred sights although she never knew or so

you believed and the light now from that high
window shines warmly and the Crucified on the
cross above the altar seems to be asleep in His
death but your faith and your hope cling to His
side as you rub the rosary Christ with your thumb
and finger and smile at the smoothness of the
touch and want no more the touch of men or the
feel of them but only the sight of Christ there
before you hung high with the sunlight pouring
over His shoulder and you reminding yourself of
the kiss of your father's lips and how he always
knew your time of month and the day of kiss and
tell was far from you as your mother's sleep was
long and sweet at least to her and you kissing the
rosary remember your mother's dark death and
the smell of rotting flesh in the room where she
died and the scent of almonds lingering in the
passages of your home until your father in his
desperate need sank with you in your mother's
bed and listened to the ghostly sighs all night
while your father's hand invaded the sacred
spoils of the childhood days but the nuns entering
the church know nothing of this or that and best
left so you think as the bell from the cloister
settles down to the midday hour and the chant

begins to sound around the dark walls of the church and the memories of your father's deeds settle down in the memory's mire and you hold your book of prayers to your eye's view and let the words come tumbling out and rise and fall to the chant's call and you remember your mother's smell and the look in her eyes as she sang the blues of her youth and slowly but painfully and outwardly dies and the sunlight peers through the high windows and settles on your book and the pages littered with words and words that suck up to your eyes and into your mind and heart and the bell and the scent and the memories sink you down to the nun's lot of prayer and lost ness in the old world's sight and you touching the edge of the book welcome the day's kiss and the dark night's touch.

Mass.

The mass is over, said Sister Margaret, *and the priest has gone. There is stillness in the church and the sweet incense lingers. The brightness*

from the sunlight filters through the stained-glass
windows and falls upon the polished wooden
floor. I can still taste my Lord upon my tongue,
and sense His energy race through my veins,
urging me on and that be done and prayers be
said and work be undertaken though it be against
the will and grain. I stare at the crucifix above
the altar, see the Crucified tortured hanging
there, bloodied and bruised, and seemingly
forsaken. If I'd been there, I would have watched
as others did and cried, and wanted to do more,
but could have done nothing, but stare or gape
loose mouthed by the shocking horror of it all. I
lower my eyes like one who has betrayed, like
one who just gaped and gazed lifting no finger to
prevent or raise a voice in protestation. I look at
my hands like one who seems to see blood
seeping through fingers and stain the nails. The
incense seeps into the nostrils; the echo of long
ago cries vibrates in the ears. I would want to
hold and embrace my Crucified, whisper to Him
on my lonely bed, or on my bended knees, before
Him say, all the love I have and feel and wish
Him to know and knowing love me back. I brush
my tongue upon the roof of my mouth where my

*Lord lingered just now, but now has gone. I am
filled with Him; He enters me and flows through
and into me like some overpowering sense,
feeling, and higher being. I am unworthy of this
love and sense of worth that feeling and thoughts
bring to me here. I have betrayed and betray still
each lingering moment of life. Each breath I take
or exhale is tainted with the touch of sin and filth
of humanness and human's frailty. Even if I
thrashed myself to death and squeezed out all my
breath, still I would not warrant one moment of
His time or love or motion of His hand upon my
wounds or tainted flesh, but He is here, beside
me, in me, over me, flowing into me, entering
each particle of my being without my knowing or
ever seeing. And even if I could know and touch
Him so near, and feel His presence close and his
whispered words so clear, still I would not
deserve such love as His, nor His firm embrace
or still gaze or gape at His tortured flesh and His
human face, for I am the lowliest of His maids;
stained with sins, full of filth of frail humanity,
and yet, and yet, He comes again, and enters me
and fills me with His love and grace, that I raise
my eyes and see His blessed and holy face. The*

mass is ended. I go in peace to serve and love my groom.

Sister Augustine's Visitor.

Sister Augustine could still hear Father Woodworth's homily in her ears as she walked steadily along the cloister towards the refectory after Mass. It had been better than his usual half-hour long dirges; it had stirred something within her: a memory almost forgotten.

There's a visitor wishing to see you in the visitor's parlour, Sister Augustine, said Sister Gregory as she approached the septuagenarian nun as she neared the refectory. Sister Augustine, her recollection disturb, stopped and frowned at the portly nun standing before her, breathing heavily as if she'd trekked miles instead of yards on her mission.

Me? A visitor for me? Sister Augustine queried sceptically.

Yes, the Portress said, *a man.*

The senior nun pulled a face and snorted mildly. *What man?* Sister Augustine asked brusquely.

He said his name was Miller, replied the portly nun. She turned and gestured for the other nun to follow her. *Elderly gentleman, neatly dressed,* Sister Gregory added. The two nuns walked the short distance to the visitor's parlour where a man stood the other side of the grille gazing at a copy of Raphael's The Ansidei Madonna.

Sister Augustine entered the parlour with uncharacteristic unease. The man turned and momentarily they stood and stared at each other in silence. Sister Augustine moved to the seat on her side of the grille and sat down; she gestured to the man to do likewise.

I thought you were dead, Sister Augustine said solemnly.

The man sat down without taking his eyes away from the elderly nun.
Reported missing, presumed dead, the man said gravely. You still have those deep eyes, Monica, he added, attempting a smile.

Sister Augustine did not smile; she stared at the man with a sense of bewilderment. *Fifty-six years is a long time to suddenly reappear from the dead, Leonard*, she said. Leonard gestured with his head as if agreeing, but said nothing. *Anyway, the Monica you knew is dead, dead to the world at least,* she added, looking away from him.

Silence came between them for a few minutes and they sat looking at each other in an uneasiness that seemed to fill the parlour like an unpleasant odour. Then Leonard spoke and Sister Augustine answered.
The conversation went from one to the other like a disagreeable game of tennis between two players, each wanting to defeat and dismiss the other as soon as possible. The conversation drew to a close and the man rose from his chair, nodded politely and walked away without turning round for a final look. Sister Augustine watched him go, and then, shaking her head, she walked slowly out of the parlour and made her way back towards the church for the office of Terce, just as the bells were tolled.

A visitor for Sister Augustine? said Sister Henry, holding her mug of coffee and slice of brown bread, uncertain which to consume first.

Yes, Sister Gregory replied, *a man.*

What man would Sister Augustine know, she's been here since 1946, informed Sister Perpetua, slicing the loaf of bread vigorously.

We all have past histories, exclaimed Sister Luke. *One of the missionary sisters I worked with in Africa had once been an unsavoury chorus-girl, her words not min*e, I may add.

I can't see Sister Augustine as a chorus-girl, said Sister Martha. *Unsavoury or otherwise.*

Perhaps he's a man friend she had years ago, mused Sister Rose audibly, nibbling at her brown bread, like a timid field mouse.

Sister Elizabeth began slicing some bread, but didn't comment on her novice sister's suggestion. She looked innocently at the assistant infirmarian who stood next to her pouring herself a mug of coffee.

Maybe it's her brother, suggested Sister
Scholastica soberly.

She doesn't have a brother, Sister Henry
informed, looking at her mug momentarily as if it
might have a clue to the mystery man.

*Well, Sister Augustine's visitor is no real concern
of ours, unless she wishes to inform u*s, Sister
Scholastica stated gently, gazing at each of the
sisters in turn. The small group of nuns nodded,
but didn't comment. Each thought their thoughts
and kept them, at least momentarily, to
themselves, as they silently consumed their
coffee and slices of brown bread.

The morning seemed to drag by and Sister
Augustine couldn't get the memory out of her
mind no matter how hard she tried to engage
herself in reading. Leonard Miller's return, even
if briefly, had disturbed her more than she was
willing to admit. She slammed the book down on
her desk in her cell and sat looking at it as if it
had somehow, directly or indirectly, defeated
her. Looking away from the book, she stared at
the crucifix on the wall above her bed and
sighed. *So long ago, yet, deep down, the pain and
guilt are still there,* she said to herself in a voice

just above a whisper. And for a few minutes she recalled the young girl she had been and the mistakes made. She stood up from her desk and slowly walked to the window and glanced down into the cloister. She suspected that her visitor was known to all of the community now, if Sister Gregory was up to her usual standard. *The tongues would wag, oh yes, she admitted to herself, even here, tongues could wag, and eyes would turn on her out of curiosity* when she entered the church for the office of Sext. *But what could she tell them? It was too long ago and too painful to recount to the mere curious. Yet she felt she had to confide in someone. But to whom could she confide?* She sighed again and hearing the bell tolling for Sext, she steadily made her way from her cell, along the cloister to the church, with her mind trying to drive back the memory to the dark corner it had been drawn from some hours before.

The way Sister Augustine looked during Sext and lunch, made Sister Scholastica seek her out after they had left the refectory. She found her wandering round the cloister garth in deep thought, stopping now and again to stare at the flowers.

Am I disturbing you, Sister Augustine? Sister Scholastica asked as she came beside the senior nun. Sister Augustine looked up from the flowers and gazed at the sister by her side.

Do I look disturbed? the septuagenarian nun replied, searching the eyes of the younger nun before her.

Yes, Sister Scholastica said, you do. She paused for a few seconds. *Anything to do with your visitor this morning?*

Sister Augustine frowned and sniffed. She turned her gaze back to the flowers.
I see Sister Gregory is as good as ever, Sister Augustine said sternly. *I suppose everyone is intrigued by my visitor and full of ideas as to whom it may have been?*

Sister Scholastica nibbled her lower lip for a couple of seconds as she looked at the back of the elderly nun. *That's human nature, I suppose. Even here, we do not cease to be human, although we may endeavour to escape its limitations and errors with the grace of God,* Sister Scholastica informed quietly.

Some may do, Sister Scholastica, some may do, Sister Augustine stated cynically. She looked up from the flowers again and stared at the young nun. *You are one of the few,* she added a little warmly.

She moved forward ploddingly as if pondering on a profound philosophical question or theological mystery. Sister Scholastica moved on beside her in silence. After wandering round to the garth entrance, they walked along the cloister and sat down in a secluded area in strained silence. After a few more seconds, Sister Augustine sighed and laid her hands on her knees. *I need to confide in someone,* she said suddenly. *You are possibly one of the few I could really trust to say nothing afterwards,* she added gravely.

Should you not confess to Father Woodworth? Sister Scholastica said.

No, the elderly nun replied firmly. *It's not absolution I require, but a human being who may have the depth of understanding and love to share the burden of another.* Her words were passionate and came from deep within. *Will you be that human being, sister?*

Sister Scholastica nodded and smiled. *Of course. Whatever you confide to me will remain with me.* The elderly nun stared at the young sister and smiled.

My visitor this morning was a man named Leonard Miller. In 1943, he was a G.I. over here in England and we became very fond of each other. My parents had been killed in an air raid in 1940 and I lived with an aunt until I joined the Land Army. We met when he was stationed nearby... She paused for a few moments. Then hesitantly she continued with her story, stopping only now and again for breath. After she had confided all that she needed to relate she sat hunched as if drained of all emotion and physical strength. The two nuns sat in silence and watched as birds hopped on the grass of the garth.

Sister Augustine placed the book back on the shelf of the library. She could not concentrate. Her mind was running over and over again the visit of Leonard Miller that morning. *What he didn't know wouldn't harm him*, she mused darkly, moving slowly across to a window that was near by. Only the priest whom she had confessed to fifty-six years before and Sister Scholastica now knew about the baby she had lost. A miscarriage *had come as both a relief and* *a shock. She had only just heard a few days before, t*hat Leonard had been reported missing presumed dead. *And I* felt such guilt and grief, Sister Augustine confessed to herself as she looked down from the window into the woods below. *Sister Scholastica seemed to taken all this in without judgement or any sign of condemnation,* she *mused, letting her eyes run over the scene beneath her.* I could have told no one else, she added to herself, closing her eyes momentarily, no one else. And she stood there in the library with her eyes closed, her hands hidden away beneath her black habit and her lips mouthing a silent prayer.

Sister Scholastica knelt down in her place in the choir stalls of the silent church and breathed in the peacefulness of the late afternoon. She recalled the conversation she had had with Sister Augustine after lunch as they sat in the cloister. Her mind sieved through the words that the elderly nun had confided to her, selecting certain aspects of the conversation and contemplating upon each in turn with her own compassion and understanding. It must have taken considerable courage for her to confess all this to me, Sister Scholastica said to herself as she lifted her eyes to the coloured-glass windows of the abbey church. She wondered how the senior nun had managed to come to terms with the apparent loss of the man she had loved in the war and the miscarriage of their baby a few days later. And then to carry this burden around with her all these years and, then, suddenly, the man whom she thought was dead comes back into her life fifty-six years later having no knowledge of the pain that had been endured. I hope, Sister Scholastica mused gravely, that she can now let all this rest with God and let this Mr Miller return to the world from where he came. She hoped so. She was sure the elderly nun would, in her own way, place the burden of grief and guilt into the hands God and resume her vocation with her usual tenacity and courage.

Sister Augustine left the refectory after supper in a slow ponderous manner. She walked along the cloister huddled against the cold evening air that blew across the garth.

May I walk with you, Sister Augustine? said plump young Sister Elizabeth from behind her. Sister Augustine turned round and looked long and hard at the sister who had spoken to her.

If you wish, Sister Augustine said with a mild sigh.

The two nuns walked on in silence for a few minutes each with their own thoughts and moods. After standing by the cloister wall for a couple of seconds gazing up at the evening sky, Sister Elizabeth said, *Do you think I'll ever make a good nun, Sister Augustine?*

Depends how you utilize the graces of God, Sister Augustine said brusquely. *If you've come here with the notion of becoming a saint or obtaining perfection, then you'll be sorely disappointed and will probably leave. However, if you realistic and understand your limitations and faults, then you may, with the grace of God, and the determined courage of a gladiator, become a reasonably good nun, I expec*t. The elderly nun resumed her silence as if the words were not hers, but had come from another person.

Sister Elizabeth nodded biting her lower lip. *Is that how you became such a good nun?* she asked in childlike innocence.

Sister Augustine tut-tutted quietly and turned and gazed at the plump sister beside her. *Am I a good nun, Sister Elizabeth*? she asked.

Of course you are, Sister Augustine, even I know that, Sister Elizabeth informed a little proudly. *And so motherly,* she added in a gentle voice.

The senior nun closed her eyes. She could sense a deep emotion rising within her and tears sat on the edge of her eyes. Her breathing, momentarily, became heavy and she placed her hand on the wall in front of her. *And you're so grand-daughterly*, Sister Augustine stated warmly, opening her eyes again and looking once more at the darkening evening sky. The young nun smiled and she too looked up at the growing darkness above them with only a faint moon as witness.

Climbing into her bed, Sister Augustine mused on the tiring day. She had learned things today. About Leonard Miller, about her sisters in Christ, and about herself. Leonard's words had angered her and still she did not confide in him about the lost baby. Sister Scholastica had shared her burden with compassion and understanding in a way that she herself had began to doubt existed any more. And young Sister Elizabeth had granted her a glimpse of what it may have been like to have been a grandmother and an understanding of herself that only a childlike perceptive mind could convey. *Am I good nun*? she asked herself as she pulled the bed covers to her chin. *God alone knows, sh*e reflected closing her eyes, He alone knows us better than we do ourselves. Far better, she sighed, far better.

Sister Scholastica switched off the lamp by her bed and closed her eyes to the darkness. She sensed she understood Sister Augustine better than she had before. *There was a depth to her and deep love which too often lay hidden behind a gruff exterior. But maybe now may become less hidden*, she mused as she recalled seeing the senior nun with young Sister Elizabeth after supper and both smiling at something with a warmth seldom seen between young and old. *Mayb*e, she mused, *her burden is a little lighter now and her past can be left behind with the young Monica who had departed from the world fifty-four years ago and died to all its claims and promises. Only God in His wisdom knows, she whispered in the dark, He alone knows.*

Sister Elizabeth's Dark Night of the Soul.

You hear the cloister bell ring that tells you it is
time to rise to the five o'clock dawn. You want to
lie there, wrap yourself closer in the blanket and
shut out the cold day. You see in your mind's eye
an endless series of mornings stretching onwards
and outwards. You squeeze your eyes shut for a
few moments to keep out the reality of the
morning. The bell persists. An inner voice speaks
and you reluctantly rise from the warm bed
covers and settle your feet on to the cold wooden
floor. Then you kneel down in your nightgown
and say an Ave and Pater Noster. The day starts
here; you sense it enter you.
The words leave your tongue and fill the room in
whispers and (you hope) Heaven. There is
darkness. It embraces you. You tear at its fabric,
but no light comes. Only mornings like this.
Seemingly so endless. Blackness around you as if
you're blind. Doubts whisper about you. And
then a voice from the door says: *Benedictus*. You
reply, but your words seem to lose themselves
somewhere across the room of your cell like
drowned souls.

After Matins, standing in the refectory, you
secretly gaze at your sisters in Christ as they

stand with eyes lowered to the refectory floor or eyes turned towards the brick wall and their own thoughts. The Grand Silence has kept you all apart soundless. Next to you, Sister Rose, her eyes downcast, her mind elsewhere, on God, no doubt, you hope. And across from you, Sister Jude, her eyes peering at the polished floor of the refectory as if some sign were there. You gaze childlike, unaware of breaking rules momentarily, until you turn and see Sister Perpetua glaring at you and shaking her head. You lower your head now, blushing, focusing, and you see the pattern the wooden floor makes and how polished it is and what work went into it for the sake of God.

The coldness of the church hits you as you recite the office of Lauds. Turning pages, you wish for it to end, not out of impiety, but because your body hates the cold and your mind wanders when the body aches. Next to you, Sister Rose sings out of tune and her voice stands out from the others like an exiled rebel. If only she would listen, you say to yourself, she'd hear her own sound against the choir.

Across the aisle you see Sister Thomas, her mouth wide open, her eyes closed as if in secret communion with God. You lower your eyes to the page. The black and red print blurs. All is awash as if water had drowned you. You mumble now, the sound a mere whisper, the chant a passing shadow.

After Mass, in the cloister, on your way to the novice's room, Sister Dominic stops you. *I understand you're with me today*, she says briskly. You bite your lower lip and nod. *Out in the cold, all I wanted,* you sigh inwardly, but outwardly smile weakly. *Sister Perpetua says you were best for the task*, she adds, looking past you, as if another was behind you awaiting her attention, but none is. You follow like one condemned, darkness caressing you. *Years of this*, the voice says inwardly. *Years and years and years.*

After the office of Sext as you walk slowly towards the refectory for lunch, you glance out at the cloister garth and see how the sunlight gleams on the damp grass. You remember grass damp like that when Richard, who termed you his girlfriend, took you up on the Downs early one year to show you the view. He held your hand and spoke of his wanting to act in films and on the London stage. You listened half-heartedly, staring across the vast scenery as if uncaged for the first time.

As you enter the refectory, you recall Richard wanting to kiss you that day and letting him you felt guilty because he wanted to do more and you wouldn't let him.

You bow towards the crucifix up on the wall behind the abbess's table, then cut two thin slices of bread before making your way to your table where you stand and wait for prayers to begin. When you told Richard you wanted to be a nun he stared at you as if you were unhinged and needed help. His face seems vague now and so it should, you tell yourself as grace begins and voices around you lift you away from your past.

Sister Martha says nothing as you wash up and dry the dishes. Her calm features make her seem miles away. You remember little of the readings during lunch; your mind wandered back and forth over your past like a ship caught in a storm. If only my prayers seemed real, you tell yourself as you dry the last of the plates and stack them neatly away. Your prayers seem to hang about your head unable to lift off and away, like flightless birds. Glancing at Sister Martha you wonder if you should ask her about the darkness about you. She stands before you, her hands joined together as if in a silent prayer. Her eyes settle on you for a few moments as if she knew something wanted to come from your lips. But you say nothing. You bow and leave the kitchen in silence. Sister Elizabeth, she calls as you walk along the cloister. You turn and she wanders up slowly as if time had little meaning. *I have a feeling you want to ask me something*, she says.

It's nothing, you reply. The nun in front of you frowns. Shaking her head she smiles. *Nothing, really*, you insist, but blushing now.

Nothing can be a problem, too, she says softly. *Without God in our lives there is only nothing. And if He seems absent, nothing can crowd in, even in those who try and devote themselves to God.*

You want to speak, but your lips seem sealed. Darkness, you utter, everywhere. You want to be embraced by someone and held tightly; you want to be told all will be well again and that God hears all and sees all. The nun nods.

Light will return, she says, *light will return,* and she's gone, as if in a dream.

After the office of None, standing with the other nuns in the cloister garth, cup of tea in your right hand, you move your eyes stealthily over those about you. Sister Rose is talking to Sister Perpetua, a glum look about her mouth. Sister Thomas chewing on cake, nodding to Sister Norbet, and standing just opposite you now, her eyes on you, Sister Scholastica. She moves slowly forward and bowing her head slightly, she says, *May I talk with you, later*? You wonder what she can possibly want to talk with you about, but say yes in a whisper. She moves away. You feel exposed as if suddenly you were undone and naked. The darkness closes in.

Sister Scholastica asks you to follow her and you do. She takes the path down through the woodlands to the private beach. She says nothing as you walk along beside her; she seems to be elsewhere, as if in prayer. When you come to the pebbles on the beach, she stands looking out to sea, with you beside her in silence. *Sister Martha asked me to speak with yo*u, Sister Scholastica says suddenly breaking the silence.

About what? You say.

She says you were experiencing what is termed the dark night of the soul, Sister Scholastica replies.

I feel lost and doubt my vocation, you say with a sigh. The sounds of the sea seem close and loud and above seagulls call circling. *I think I am losing my faith,* you add looking down at the pebbles.

Faith is a gift from God, Elizabeth. You have not lost it, merely
misunderstood what it means to have faith.

And what does it mean? You ask, feeling tired.

No one can have faith in God without loving Him. To love Him means to do that which He asks and to accept that which He sends you. If you have that then even if His presence seems far away, you have the essence, the heart of faith, Sister Scholastica informs gently.

*But nothing seems to get through to God as far as I can see. My prayers seem unanswer*ed; *my daily routine seems pointless; my vocation to be a nun seems to be a mistake.* You pause. Tears feel close. Staring ahead at the sea you continue: *All around me is darkness. I feel as if my life is empty and getting emptier each day.*
And God seems to have abandoned me, you say still staring straight ahead.

Do you want to leave St Benedict's? Sister Scholastica asks in a voice so soft it makes you want to cry. You shake your head in negation. *Even the great saints had times of spiritual darkness. T.S. Eliot says that darkness declares the glory of the light. Our love of God is an act of faith which clings to Him no matter how we feel or what we experience,* she smiles and touches the sleeve of your habit. *God is here; He always is. If He seems absent, He is merely testing your love and thereby your faith, Elizabeth.* She stops and gazes at you. You see only a blurred image of her. Tears fill your eyes. She embraces you as a mother would a pained child. And you hear her gentle words about you soothing as a soft kiss.

After the office of Vespers you remain in the church kneeling in your place in choir. The words of Sister Scholastica echo within you, but the darkness is still there. Sister Luke is up by the altar moving things about in her tasks. She seems far away like God. You stare at her for a few minutes, then close your eyes. You remember Richard saying *that faith in some holy cause was a substitute for our lost faith in ourselves.* He seemed so confident in his statement as if you were a wayward child needing his guidance. Behind your closed eyes, kneeling with head bowed, you sense no regret of leaving him behind. He wanted more from you than you were prepared to give. And that day when you let him kiss you, he wanted more and you refused. He said coldly that chastity was the most unnatural of sexual perversions. After that there was silence between you and it all seemed to end that day his fondness for you such as it was.

Are you busy, Sister Elizabeth? Sister Luke says breaking you from your thoughts, not prayers.

No, sorry, Sister... You stand and gaze at her. She stares at you with her stern eyes. Her mouth seems fixed tight as if talking was an effort.

Sister Perpetua says you can aid me in the sacristy, she says.

You follow her down the aisle, crossing yourself as you go. You feel tired, wish for bedtime and sleep, and hope the darkness will soon end. In the sacristy Sister Luke points to this and that, and tells you where such and such goes, and what is used by the priest and when and why. Her hands, you notice, have a certain poise in their motion.

You watch her hands as they move from task to task like dancers in movement. Her features have a fixed but calm concentration about them as they perform the tasks as if each task were a prayer. *To pray is to work, to work is to pray* one of the old nuns had told you once. And here you tell yourself is the proof. You never noticed before.

Thank you, Elizabeth, she says suddenly. Her face lights up. *You have done well. You can go now; I think your Latin classes are due.* Sister Luke nods her head for you to leave and her features become fixed again. Like doors closing. Like a light turned off.

As you sit in your cell reading after Compline you think about Sister Scholastica's words. Darkness is still about you. Each task an effort; each word of prayer fruitless. Even reading tires you. You close the book and walk to the window. Outside it is getting dark and the cloister is only lit here and there by small lights giving off shadows that disappear into blackness. You watch as Sister Gregory plods along the cloister in and out of the darkness and then vanishes from sight like a vague ghost. You wonder if maybe that was like you and your faith: in and out of the darkness and then one day vanishing into the blackness without word or warning. You close your eyes and hope the darkness does glorify the light and God there loving you.

SISTER LUCY'S DEPARTURE.

Sister Teresa kneels in the choir stall after Compline. She can still hear the bell for the angelus ringing in her ears. *Just an hour ago*, she muses, *just an hour ago, she was there in front of me, awaiting my embrace and kiss for her leave taking, as all the sisters who were there outside the refectory had done. Only I wanted to give her more than a brief embrace and kiss on the cheek. She knew, too, but what could we do? Off to Rome. For how long? She didn't know. Couldn't say. Sister Lucy off to Rome,* Sister Ambrose had said proudly one afternoon three weeks ago in the recreation room as they sat knitting, reading, or other such things in common. *Off to Rome?* the sisters had said. But none had felt it like she and Lucy had. A sword in the breast more like. Lucy had wept. *But what could she do? How long was it to be?* she had asked Mother Abbess. *Who knows my child*, Mother had replied. *No way of it putting off. No way out. The Lord calls; the Lord sends*, mother had said softly, yet firmly. Wept both of us very much those few precious moments alone. *There are only three of us left in the church now*, Sister Teresa tells herself, looking up briefly and glancing opposite at the two sisters on their knees. *Young Sister Maria looks almost purity itself*, Sister Teresa muses as she looks at the young nun, eyes closed, stiff and upright in her white habit. *And old Sister Bonaventure, so rumour, yes, rumour, even here there are rumours, has it, likes to be the last in church after Compline so she can lock the church door behind her. But what do they feel about Sister Lucy?* Sister Teresa asks herself, lowering her eyes and moving her knees briefly to stop the numbness coming, as it does after awhile. *Just an hour ago. We had waited for that moment. Dreaded it even. Now it's gone. And by the morning, she'll be off to the airport and away.* Sister Teresa moves forward; touches the floor with her right hand to steady herself. *God, how long do you require Lucy? Couldn't you have called some other sister? No, sorry Lord, that's not my place to ask. It's just that it pains me so much her going. Pains very much her going away. Pains us both, Lucy and me, her having to go to Rome. No more seeing her in choir in the mornings or evenings or other times of the Office. No more in the refectory or in the cloister to see her smiling face. To have to face all that without her being there is just unthinkable, but now a fact. But maybe if I get up early and wait by the cloister, I may just catch a glimpse as she leaves. But what good will that do? Can't break the Grand Silence and say goodbye. And what would Sister Thomas say, who, no doubt, will be the one to drive Lucy to the airport? Just a glimpse. Just a last glance from each to each. Maybe a final smile.* Sister Maria rises from her knees, and moving slowly, goes out into the aisle, genuflecting to the altar. *Saying goodnight to Our Lord*, Sister Teresa muses sadly, as she watches the young nun walk slowly down towards the lower door. *Which leaves just Sister Bonaventure and me*, Sister Teresa tells herself, glancing quickly over to the old nun who kneels motionless with her eyes closed as if asleep or dead. *Just over an hour ago now. Should have said whatever I wanted in a low whisper, but I didn't, just kissed her and embraced her as the others did, as if it meant no more than another sister going to Rome. To Rome.* And she sees in her mind's eye, Sister Lucy a few feet away on her side of the choir. A few feet away. Could almost touch her. But it is all in the mind. This is where she will remain until she returns some years hence. Years? How can we *bear years? Months would have been bad enough…Weeks, days, hours. God. I shall not stand it here without her. Her tall slim figure gliding here and there. Her pale-blue eyes glancing at me in choir. Here.*

Looking up she sees the old nun sit back on her choir seat. Silent and now motionless. *Perhaps I had better go, leave old Sister Bonaventure to her task. I wonder if she ever felt about another sister as I do about Lucy? Doubt it. No probably not.* And watching the old nun open her eyes, Sister Teresa rises from her knees and moves out into the aisle. *Lord, if only it wasn't Lucy. Someone else. Some other nun.* She moves towards the door. At the end of the aisle, she turns and looks down towards the altar. The old nun moves up and turns off the lights one by one. Darkness gradually follows her. Sister Teresa turns, goes out the door, up the steps, and into the cloister. Stillness and a chill in the air. Moving to the edge of the cloister, she looks up at the night sky. Moon and stars bright tonight, she thinks sadly, letting her hand brush against the wall. *Over there in that cell*, she whispers and gestures with her head and finger, *Lucy sleeps perhaps or waits unable to sleep. Dreams or thinks of me maybe*? she whispers again now. *Hush now or Sister Bonaventure will creep behind you and think you're out of your head*, Sister Teresa muses darkly. Moving slowly along the cloister, she watches the cell as if it were the center of the universe. A slim, barely seen slither of light seeps through the wooden shutters of the cell. *She is awake still*, Sister Teresa mutters to herself inwardly. *Awake and waiting. Should I go and see? Spirit within is weak. Lack courage.* Moving along the cloister, she senses the old nun behind her. Old eyes, lowered head unturning, the old nun passes. As if I should not be here. I should be long in my cell by now. *Normally I would no doubt. Lucy I am here,* she mouths to the cell. *I am here, Lucy,* she whispers. She stops, stares, and waits. *Why*? she asks. *For what? For what?* Along the cloister again, she moves as if in a dream. Up the cold stone stairs to the upper building. *We met here that first time,* Sister Teresa remembers, standing still briefly, as the memory lingers. *Yes, here,* she says to her inmost being. *Here we stood, and for a few moments were wordless and just smiled. What it was captured us we never could tell. Didn't know. Just felt it. Knew only that.* She sighs and feels like weeping. But braces herself. *We first kissed where?* she asks herself, climbing the stairs slowly. Remembering now, she smiles through tears. Yes, the stairs leading down to the crypt. One evening. Darkness about them. Briefly, lips together in the darkness met. Remembers now. Wants to weep. Loudly. *Yes, so that all the whole community will know.* But she doesn't. She weeps quietly and to herself. The landing where Sister Lucy's cell is. Mine down passed hers. *Should I just knock and say a last farewell? Just a few seconds? Knock*? She moves to the cell door and stands looking at it. Her hand forms a small fist and she lingers over the wooden panels. But her nerves give way and she moves back. *What will she say? What will Sister Lucy say?* she asks inwardly. *What if she's asleep? Needs her rest for tomorrow.* She moves to the door again and lifts her fist. She numbs and begins to shake. Her fist skims the surface of the wooden panels. She barely feels the wood. Touches it gently with her palm now. Places it on the wooden panels and smoothes it downwards. *I am here*, she mouths to the woodenness of the door. She lets her head rest against the panels. Her eyes close. If only thoughts could speak instead of lips, she thinks and mouths again the words*: Lucy I am here.* But no one comes; the door remains closed. Opens her eyes. Tears blind her now. She sees nothing but a blur of watery shapes. Raises her hand again and lets it brush against the woodenness once more. Clenches her hand tight and forms a fist. Raises it over the wooden panels and taps gently a Morse code of sorts. Movement on the other side of the door freezes her. Sister Teresa moves away, stands shaking. The door latch rises and Sister Lucy opens the door slowly. She looks and stares at a shaking, pale-faced, Sister Teresa. Gesturing with her hand she beckons the shaking sister inwards. Closes the door and the passageway is empty once more. Together they stand, each looking at the other in silence. No words. Just eyes looking and seeking answers. Sister Teresa wants to say what her heart screams out inside to say, but says nothing. Sister Lucy, tall and slim of frame, tries to say, but words won't come. Dumbness holds them both. Putting out a hand, Sister Teresa attempts to touch, but then pulls back her hand and hides it in her habit. The other watches and lifts her hands outwardly as if to share all that she has which is all that there is to see. Her eyes move from the other's face to her hands hidden. Sister Lucy walks over to the table and picking up a pencil writes on a torn piece of paper, *what is it you want of me?* The other nun stares at the message. Then taking the pencil from the other's hand writes: *I want to say a last farewell.* Their eyes meet. A smile appears on Sister Lucy's lips. She opens her arms and gestures for the other to come. Sister Teresa wipes her eyes with her hand. She enters the embrace and sinks into the arms. Senses herself being held tightly and then feels a kiss on her cheek and lifts her head and sees, through a slightly blurred vision, the smile she thought she'd not see again. She closes her eyes. All is silent. Emptiness about her. And when she opens her eyes, she is standing outside the door with her fist raised. The door is closed. The woodenness appears hard. *Have I dreamt all that?* she asks herself, tearfully letting her fist brush against the surface. *No kiss. No embrace. No message.* Just then, the door opens and Sister Lucy stands, tall and slim, in silence. Her eyes scan about her and then settle on Sister Teresa. She stares and mouths words that do not come. She moves out her hand and feels for the other's hand. Touching. Feeling. Mouths again words. Gestures with her hands. The sisters enter the cell together in silence. They embrace and kiss. The light becomes darkness. The passageway is still and empty. To Rome. Sister Lucy. And who knows if she will. Tomorrow is another day.

BEFORE PRIME.

Sister Pius can still sense the taste of coffee on her tongue from breakfast with the slice of brown bread with a thin spread of butter as she turns over the page of the book on contemplation written by some unknown Carthusian nun the words momentarily failing to reach her the

message left on the page the thought of the next
meal already making her mouth moisten and the
smell of fresh made coffee tempting her nose
bringing to mind the first time she had come to
the convent as a guest and young girl full of
enthusiasm for the idea of being a nun much to
her parent's disquiet especially her mother who
had wanted and been looking forward to
grandchildren even though Eve as she was then
had never been interested in boys or that side of
things but her mother had said that would come
she would find Mr Right and that side of things
would come naturally implying Sister Pius muses
now that being a nun was unnatural against
nature and only the oddities in the world would
want to be shut away from the world and men
and their families and the prospect of marrying
and having children and there had been the rows
and the tempers frayed and the words said in
haste and even on the day she entered her mother
had not come around to the idea even if her
father had accepted the fait accompli rather
grudgingly and in all the years she had been in
the convent her parents had not written once not
a word just the one visit her father made looking
at her as they spoke as if she had grown another
head or caught a dreadful disease and had said
her mother couldn't bring herself to visit the
place her daughter had died in and those words

hurt the way her father had just come out with them the place her daughter had died in and yet she had her secrets too the things she had never told her parents especially her mother never mentioned once that her Uncle Randolph her mother's brother had molested her one summer while she was staying with him and Aunt Grace while her parents were off on some tour of Europe and as she places her hand on the page of the book in front of her she can still feel his hands on her still sense his breath on her that smell of beer and tobacco and the roughness of his unshaven face as she leaned over her and as the memory returns again she closes the book with a small slam and the echo of it fills the room disturbs a paper on the table in front of her and the memory still fresh the deeds done so embedded deeply that she doesn't think it will ever go that it will ever leave and she had not said a word about that summer to anyone not even her mother not even to make a point about what men could do even those who were supposed to be close to you and yet she never did never said one word about him and the things he had done and taking a deep sigh she gets up from the chair and walks to the window looking down on the cloister garth and the mulberry tree that is now full of fruit and can see birds in the branches and a nun walking along the cloister ready to pull the bell for the office of Prime and even now she dislikes the smell of apples the smell of them cooking or the smell of apples being stored because apples she associates with him and the place he took her and the things he did and it was apples she could smell as he touched her and interfered with her and the scent of apples in the air as he leaned over her and looking down again into the cloister the nun has gone and the early morning sun is coming over the cloister wall and the bell is being tolled for Prime and making the sign of the cross she pushes the memory of him and his deeds and that summer back into the depths of her mind closes the door on it in the room in her brain's memory cells and looking up at the Crucified on the wall above her bed with the features of the Christ battered by time and its hands she nods her head and looks away taking in her mind the image of Him and perhaps a sense of peace and the fact that she is a bride after all a bride of Christ married to one who would not molest or hurt or say cruel words or betray and where no smell of apples will spoil her day.

AFTER LAUDS.

Moving from the church after Lauds to the cloister Sister Lucia walks at the required pace taking in the statue of Our Lady with the flowers in the clay pots around the base the Child Jesus in her arms the flowers fresh the scent reaching up to her nose the memory of the Christ hanging from the crucifix with one arm in her parent's room at home the arm broken off at the elbow her mother claiming that father did it in one of his rages threw across the room she had said and the Sacred Heart of Jesus high on the wall of the room with the eyes of the Crucified staring down at her making her feel the sense of sin as a child and her mother pulling her before it and making her kneel down with the small rosary and recite the sorrowful mysteries over and over until the finger and thumb were raw and passing now she lets her fingers touch the top of the wall of the cloister garth the roughness the fingers sensing the brick's the roughness and looking up seeing the mulberry tree in the corner of the cloister noticing the early morning birds the birdsong the wind moving branches and remembering the first time she had seen the square area of sky of the cloister gazing up with the stars and moon like a framed picture that first time visiting the convent and Sister Josephine saying that is our piece of Heaven and keeping those words close to her heart she ascends the stairs to her cell(our cell

Sister James had said years back the nun has no
personal property her vow of poverty forbids it)
and climbing the stairs she notices a dead
butterfly on the window ledge a Red Admiral
lying there lifeless the colours still held and
looking up saw the cobweb hanging from the
corner and knowing that Mother Abbess if she
saw it would be unhappy and so taking a few
moments wipes it away with a brush of her hand
and rubs her hands together to clear away the
dead matter and the taking in the air waiting for a
few moments to gather thoughts she remembers
the time she had to climb the stairs back and
forth as a novice after Sister Lawrence had see
her run down to get to Lauds on time and made
her ascend and descend three times until she had
learnt the rule about walking never to run never
to rush and pushing the memory aside she walks
up to the landing and makes her way along the
passage way to her cell door which she opens
and enters in closing the door behind her and
leaning her back against it feeling the hard wood
touching her backbone the flesh feeling the
hardness through the black serge cloth and
turning her eyes she sees the crucifix on the wall
above the bed and the bed made neat and precise
the pillow positioned exact the bedside cabinet
containing her prayer book her notebook for
faults the chamber pot for nights the small lamp

and across the room the window where morning
light was beginning to show and the shutters
pushed back and the sky becoming lighter and to
the right of that the table and bowl and water jug
and the white towel and soap and the water cold
and the soap almost scentless and walking away
from the door she picks up her Bible and sits at
the desk on the chair opening the book and
allowing her eyes to scan the pages taking in the
text finding the right passages Lectio Divina
Sister James had said that first day in the convent
passing her the Bible showing her pages and
bringing her the Rule of St Benedict and the
nun's fingers so thin and so white turning the
pages the hand holding so gently carefully and
allowing the memory to drift off she looks up to
the painting on the wall above the bookcase the
Sacred Heart of Jesus the hand bent slightly the
finger pointing to the heart surrounded by thorns
the look in the eyes gazing the eyes of the
Crucified the look the hurt there the pain sensed
the agony felt and she recalls the picture in her
parent's room her knees aching where her mother
had forced her to kneel to recite the sorrowful
mysteries over and over and closing her eyes she
senses her mother's ghostly hand on her shoulder
sensing shivers down her spine hearing the
whispering voice about her shoulder the warm
breath the memory of her mother's last days and

painful drawn out death.

AFTER MASS.

The nuns filed out of the church into the cloister
after mass and then dispersed and went their own
ways. Sister Martha went to the refectory, which
was almost empty except for old Sister Agatha
who nibbled brown bread like a sparrow and
young Sister Elizabeth beside her who acted as
the elderly nun's guardian angel and stood
sipping black tea from the urn in a big white
mug. Sister Martha cut a slice of brown bread
and spread butter over it and taking a white mug
downloaded black coffee from the urn on the
table and went and stood facing the wall taking
in the light from the high window. That had
captured her imagination once when she first
came to the convent back in 68. The light shining
through the window; the way it seemed like a
holy picture straight from Heaven; an inspiring
thing back then, that light, promised warmth
from a sun the other side of the pattern glass. Her
first communion on the Sunday from the hands
of the old abbess shaking from the creeping
Parkinson's that was there; the waiting for some

inner revelation, some light to switch on in her mind and soul after the receiving of the Corpus Christi on the tongue. It never came, that feeling, just faith, keep the faith, Sister Josephine had said afterwards, an outward sign of inward grace like all the sacraments, she had explained gently, knowing about fresh converts to the faith and the eagerness to experience the workings of the Holy Spirit, the voices of angels and so forth. They never came, Sister Martha mused, sipping her coffee, holding the bread and butter in her hand watching the specks of dust move in the light from the high window. No consolation of faith; no high spirits; no feeling elated; no sense that she was touching the hand of God or had His ear all to herself. Just faith, holding on in there, keeping her afloat the seas of doubt and darkness, which her father had succumbed to, that deep darkness of doubt and despair that he wore like a snug dark overcoat. She nibbled the brown bread; tasted the butter; sensed the saltiness. The salt and the sea. Down by the sea, she and Sister Josephine and two other nuns, sitting on the private beach at the far grounds of the convent throwing stones across the incoming waves, and talking amongst themselves, and she thinking about home and her father and the darkness almost drowning him and Sister Josephine looking at you and bringing you back to the conversation that entailed discussion on Wittgenstein and language and she looking over their heads at the ships going by on the horizon, wondering who was there and why and where they were going and the conversation floating by her like the soft breeze from the sea. Sister Martha sipped more coffee. Sister Elizabeth escorted the old nun from the refectory with the patience of a saint. Need it with that old dear. Moan, moan, moan like an ever-returning tide from her thin lips. They had gone. Just silence and faith and the sensation of warm coffee on the tongue and down the back of the throat warm and cosy like a mother's kiss.

AFTER MATINS.

There's a chill in the six o'clock cloister Sister Catherine feels as she walks from the church to the refectory her fingers brushing against the rough brickwork along the top of the knee-high wall around the cloister pausing momentarily to gaze at the mulberry tree in the garth to see the birds there then she lowers her eyes to the frost on the grass the whiteness mingling with the green the sharp chill biting the fingers the wind hurting her cheeks as her mother's hand did once when she slapped her for kissing the Murphy boy next door in the porch after a party and the memory of the sharp slap still remains in her mind like a scar on flesh and her mother saying boys like him are only after one thing and once they get it they move on to some other slut and the anger in her mother's eyes stung her more than the hand slap and looking up the sky promises more chill the white frost on the rooftops of the convent and the bell tower and dark rooks in the far off trees and looking back to the cloister she sees Sister Dominic pacing along head down hand clutching the rosary hanging from the black belt the fingers rubbing the dark wooden beads and her voice mumbling softly and so Sister Catherine enters the refectory smelling straight away the fresh baked bread the hot coffee from the urn on the oak table the polish from the floors the cooking from the kitchen and cutting a slice of brown bread with the sharp knife and pouring black coffee into the large white mug she walks to the table by the high windows and faces the wall taking in the brown red brickwork the light from the high windows falling gently like snow on the surrounding air and nibbling the bread she wants to sense God's presence needs to allow space for Him but senses only the chill of morning the

hunger being slowly appeased the warmth of the
coffee mug entering her fingers the coldness in
her toes beginning to ease and lifting her eyes to
the window above her head she remembers her
mother dragging her to confessions to tell the
priest all tell Father Cassidy everything you bad
girl tell him every last thing you and that boy
Murphy did do you hear me and her mother's
voice awakens in her mind every word and
presses against the walls of her brain and the
memory fresh as eggs new laid and her mother's
fat fingers pinching deep into her skin leaving
red marks the pain of the slapped behind still
there deep in her mind and gazing down she
looks at her hand holding the mug the steam
from the coffee rising like incense at mass like
prayers said and turning around looks over and
above the abbess's table at the crucifix on the
wall the Crucified pinned to the stained wood the
nails embedded deeply in the hands and the
hands like shells the fingers pointing inwards His
face chiselled with hurt the blue painted eyes
looking Heavenward a sadness there a rejection a
pained expression touching her reminding her of
her mother's last stare when she entered the
convent and looked back at her standing in the
convent parlour and saw that cold glare that
seemed to say so you have left me alone to face
old age you selfish girl you are just like your

father just like him and lifting the coffee mug to
her lips and sipping the liquid she closes her eyes
to the hanging Christ and the memories that
linger and like the chill in flesh and feet they hurt
her still.

BEFORE MASS.

The priest crossed the cloister garth of the
convent watched from a high window by Sister
Martha. Wonder where he's going to now?
Church probably to prepare for mass. There's a
bald patch on the top of his head; no matter how
he combs it, it still shows through. Father's hair
was like that, but brown and wavy with the odd
curl. He'd let me comb his hair when I was a girl.
Let me do what ever I liked with it. His little
hairdresser he called me. And there was that
patch of baldness; no matter how I combed it it
was still there. Then I got too old to comb his
hair and he became odd, moaned, and said cruel
things. Then his mind fell apart and he was gone
and another man took his place although he
looked the same. Mother had no patience with

him and finally he was put away in a home with others equally odd, miserable, and smelling of urine. Sister Martha watched until the priest had gone from sight. He had made footprint in the snow. Right across the whiteness he'd left dark stains where his feet had trod. Birds gathered looking for food. She watched the sky. White. Brilliant white. No sign of clouds or sun; just the snow covered buildings of the convent and the tree in the cloister garth. Coldness bit at her flesh. She rubbed her hands together. Flesh on flesh. Warmth. Flesh on her flesh. Robert had kissed her once behind the bike sheds at school. She had not resisted although Mother said that she ought to have done. Gives boys the wrong idea Mother had said. Robert never did it again. Maybe he didn't like to or maybe other girls gave him the wrong ideas better. Sister Martha sighed. The room was cold. The small fireplace where she was permitted to light a fire on winter days was out. She'd light it later after mass. She went from the window and stood in front of her crucifix on the wall. The Crucified hung silent and stiff and dust had gathered behind His head. She'd have to take it down and clean the dust away. After mass maybe. There was a cobweb hanging from one of the arms. Must clean it up and dust it down. Mother's crucifix hung above her bed. It must have seen some sights at night.

Father and mother were always doing things in their room I remember hearing as a child. The bed springs going. Mother's voice. Father was well then. Seemed so. Stood outside their room one night wanting water too frightened to knock so I just stood waiting for the sound to stop. Mother was laughing. Then they both laughed. The coldness was all around me so I returned to bed snuggling down to get warm again. The Crucified hung waiting for death. Father waited in his darkness. Mother never visited in the end. No point she said. He doesn't know me. Sister Martha sighed and walked to the table and took out her breviary from the drawer. Time for mass soon. Cold church. Cold choir stalls. The heating not working. Only the fire in the common room to warm the hands. She held the breviary tight in her hands. Rubbed the leather binding. Ora pro nobis, she muttered. Pray for us. She opened the door and looked down the passageway. No one about, the other nuns must have left for church already. She closed her door softly with a light click. The echo of the click followed her along the passageway until all was silent once more.

PRIOR TO LAUDS.

Sister Luke spreads the bed cover down flat with
the palm of her hand sensing the roughness on
her skin taking in the dark brown colour the way
it fits neatly into the sides of the bed and at the
end just as her mother had shown her years back
like an envelope tucked in neat and tidy no ends
hanging out no odds and sods her father would
have said then standing back she looks quickly
around the room taking note of the crucifix on
the wall above the bed with the cross she'd made
with the palm leaf folded small and placed
behind the back and shoulders of the Christ with
the face tortured and eyes closed and the
bloodied crown of thorns and the thin pins nailed
into the plaster hands and feet and remembers the
crucifix her parents had above the bed with a
rosary hanging down and the Crucified (as her
father called Him) looking distraught and old and
haggard and pictures of saints on the walls and
the smell of perfume and body sweat and hair oil
and turning her eyes to the washstand she sees
that all is as it should be the jug placed just right
next to the white enamel bowl for washing and
the plain white towel over the wooden rail and
the soap in the dish thin and dull green and
looking over at the window sees the roof of the
guest house and the small bell tower in the

cloister which was tolled for the meal times and other less important hours and the tree in the garth with its buds and birds and sun just coming over the rooftop and the first clouds of day arriving like bridesmaids for a wedding and looking away she gazes down at her black habit brushing off the crumbs of bread from breakfast in the refectory taken standing up peering through the high windows at the sky and the sound of silence entering her like a sharp knife and putting her hand down now to the rosary that hangs from the black belt she feels the beads and rubs her thumb and finger over them moving along until she touches the wooden cross and then rubs her thumb over the Christ over His head and arms then slowly down the body and legs feeling the small Christ chilled by the morning air and then releasing it lets it fall back against the serge of black cloth and taking one last look around she opens the door of the room and goes out into the corridor pulling the door shut behind her with a dull thud just as Sister Josephine had shown her that first morning not to allow noise to disturb not to disturb the sisters not permit disorder or disruption to prayer or contemplation and walking along the corridor she thinks of the passageway of Donal's house dark and creepy with the talk of ghosts and phantoms over supper and Donal jumping out at her from

some doorway and grabbing her from behind and
kissing the nape of her neck and his arms about
her rubbing against her holding her close his
whispered words his lewd suggestions his hands
feeling her and she pushing him back and away
and wanting him gone and beginning to scream
until he put his hand over her mouth and
muttered for silence for hush for the hell she'd
wake his mother and then there'd be hell to pay
and then it was all gone as she walks to the stairs
and looks down at the descending nun walking at
the side by the wall head bowed hands tucked
away into the habit out of sight and lets her go on
and waits by the top fingering the rosary shutting
the door of memories shutting out Donal and his
hands and words and suggestions and the dark
room and the bed and then the bell rings for
Lauds breaking through the memories pushing
through the dull images allowing light to enter
the light from the windows the high windows and
the cold air enters her lungs and the voice of her
Christ bidding her come with each toll of bell
and footsteps bringing her closer to her Heaven
and miles away from that Hell.

RAPE & CRUCIFIXION.

Sister Lucia kneels down. Her knees sense the bare wooden floor. Hardness, roughness. She closes her eyes. The room is silent, the smell of polish, soap. She tries to order her thoughts. To calm them, to get them to focus. Her hands touch, the fingers entwine. Flesh on flesh. Words won't come; the words freeze in her throat. Just back in the convent after two years away in the foreign mission. She can picture it; see the mission chapel, the small house with walls, the square cloister. The chill of the room touches her. The mission had been warm, often hot. She tries to utter words, prayers. Nothing, nothing but sounds and images. She can still picture the soldiers who raped her. Still feel them inside her. She feels the hard floor beneath her knees, the knees ache, the back stiffens. She utters an Ave, that usually helps, starts her off, but nothing follows. First one soldier then the other, each smelling of sweat and drink. One dark eyed and unshaven roughly undressing her, dragging her this way and then that while the other laughed. She senses them still, senses their fingers, hands, penises, laughter. Crucified on that ground, pinned down, struggling, feeling the heat, the thrusts, the skyline above empty of all, but dull clouds. *You have not broken your vow of celibacy,* the abbess had told her in the quiet talk they'd had a few hours ago, *you never consented, you were raped my dear child.* Yes, the word clings to her like a stain, a mark, as if they'd nailed her to the ground and hammered into her until she bled. She sighs. Squeezes her fingers tight against each other. Pain, pain. A sister nun stood by the bed when the doctor examined her at the mission, his hands touching, his eyes professional, but still a man's, still looking, the sister nun blushing, averting her eyes, fingering a rosary, muttering a breathy prayer. The doctor asked her questions, felt her forehead, took her pulse, studied the bruises, the cuts, swellings. She gets up from the floor, walks to the window, and looks down at the cloister. Oh to be in England now that. She opens the window and lets in the sounds of birds, wind, trees moving. The breeze astounds her. She allows it to embrace her, finger her face, her eyes. One of the soldiers slapped her face until it went numb, her eyes stared, her lips felt swollen. *Did they?* Sister Thomas asked at the mission after the doctor had gone and made his report. *They had,* she muttered through bloated lips. *Raped and sodomized.* Sister Thomas had watery eyes. The Sister nun standing by the bed stared ahead, eyes glassy, fingering the rosary. The breeze chills her and so she closes the window and stands looking at the large wooden cross on the wall above the bed. *The cross symbolizes the I, the ego, the me, crossed out, the negation of self, the novice mistress had said years before. The denial of self, is the first step towards Christ,* she had said, pointing to the crucifix on the wall of the chapel. She rubs her hands, warms them. *What of her self?* She thought she had crossed out her self, her ego, her me. She feels them still, their entering, the laughter. Brutalized, beaten, crucified. A share in *Christ's sufferings, one nun had said at the mission. Shared in suffering. Share in. Suffering. Still. It will take time*, Sister Thomas said. *Time, ticking clock, age, death. To forgive. Forgiveness, pardon, mercy, compassion. They know not what they do. They did. They knew. God forgive mayb*e. She sits on the bed and fingers with the large beads of the rosary. Undone, feels so undone. As if they had opened her up and tore out her very being, her soul. She feels the wooden beads as she fingers them. She holds the small crucified Christ on the rosary and kisses Him, senses her flesh, feels her faith clinging on by her fingertips. *Don't let go, don't go, don't turn out the light, don't allow me to drown in the dull cold dark.*

Printed in Great Britain
by Amazon